"You smell of roses, Libby," he murmured deeply.

She could feel the sudden tautness of his lean body against her, the increasing warmth of his embrace. She tried to pull away, but he wouldn't let her.

"Don't fight this," Jordan said gruffly. "You haven't stopped wanting me."

"I want hot chocolate, too, Jordan, but it still gives me a migraine, so I don't drink it."

His dark eyebrows lifted. "Let's see if you can convince me."

He bent, drawing his lips slowly, tenderly, across her mouth in a teasing impression of a kiss. He was lazy and gentle, and after a few seconds her traitorous body betrayed her. She was lost. Her arms wreathed around his strong neck. She gave in to the delight of his ardent touch, to the mastery that she'd only guessed at before.

"I can't get enough of you, Libby!" he whispered hungrily.

She nuzzled closer, drowning in the pleasure of being close to him. She shouldn't be letting this happen. But she couldn't help herself....

Dear Reader,

Spring is here. And what better way to enjoy nature's renewed vigor than with an afternoon on the porch swing, lost in four brand-new stories of love everlasting from Silhouette Romance?

New York Times bestselling author Diana Palmer leads our lineup this month with *Cattleman's Pride* (#1718), the latest in her LONG, TALL TEXANS miniseries. Get to know the stubborn, seductive rancher and the shy innocent woman who yearns for him. Will her love be enough to corral his heart?

When a single, soon-to-be mom hires a matchmaker to find her a practical husband, she makes it clear she doesn't want a man who inspires reckless passion...but then she meets her new boss! In Myrna Mackenzie's miniseries THE BRIDES OF RED ROSE classic legends take on a whole new interpretation. Don't miss *Midas's Bride* (#1719)!

Her Millionaire Marine (#1720), from *USA TODAY* bestselling author Cathie Linz, and part of her MEN OF HONOR miniseries, finds a beautiful lawyer making sure the marine she secretly adores fulfills his grandfather's will. Falling in love with the daredevil is *not* part of the plan!

And Judith McWilliams's *Dr. Charming* (#1721) puts a stranded female traveler in the path of a mysterious doctor; she agrees to take a job in exchange for a temporary home—with him. Now, this man makes her want to explore passion, but can he tempt her to take the *ultimate* risk?

Sincerely,

Mavis C. Allen
Associate Senior Editor

Please address questions and book requests to:
Silhouette Reader Service
U.S.: 3010 Walden Ave., P.O. Box 1325, Buffalo, NY 14269
Canadian: P.O. Box 609, Fort Erie, Ont. L2A 5X3

DIANA PALMER

CATTLEMAN'S PRIDE

SILHOUETTE *Romance*®

Published by Silhouette Books

America's Publisher of Contemporary Romance

To Amy in Alabama

SILHOUETTE BOOKS

ISBN 0-373-19718-7

CATTLEMAN'S PRIDE

Visit Silhouette Books at www.eHarlequin.com

Printed in U.S.A.

Books by Diana Palmer

Silhouette Romance

Darling Enemy #254
Roomful of Roses #301
Heart of Ice #314
Passion Flower #328
‡*Soldier of Fortune* #340
After the Music #406
Champagne Girl #436
Unlikely Lover #472
Woman Hater #532
†*Calhoun* #580
†*Justin* #592
†*Tyler* #604
†*Sutton's Way* #670
†*Ethan* #694
†*Connal* #741
†*Harden* #783
†*Evan* #819
†*Donavan* #843
†*Emmett* #910
King's Ransom #971
†*Regan's Pride* #1000
†*Coltrain's Proposal* #1103
Mystery Man #1210
†*The Princess Bride* #1282
†*Callaghan's Bride* #1355
‡*Mercenary's Woman* #1444
†*Lionhearted* #1631
†*Cattleman's Pride* #1718

Silhouette Books

Silhouette Christmas Stories 1987
"The Humbug Man"

Silhouette Summer Sizzlers 1990
"Miss Greenhorn"

To Mother with Love 1993
"Calamity Mom"

Montana Mavericks
Rogue Stallion

Abduction and Seduction 1995
"Redbird"

†*A Long, Tall Texan Summer* 1997

Lone Star Christmas 1997
†"Christmas Cowboy"

Montana Mavericks Weddings 1998
"The Bride Who Was Stolen in the Night"

†*Love with a Long, Tall Texan* 1999

Steeple Hill Love Inspired
Blind Promises

Silhouette Desire

The Cowboy and the Lady #12
September Morning #26
Friends and Lovers #50
Fire and Ice #80
Snow Kisses #102
Diamond Girl #110
The Rawhide Man #157
Lady Love #175
Catleman's Choice #193
‡*The Tender Stranger* #230
Love by Proxy #252
Eye of the Tiger #271
Loveplay #289
Rawhide and Lace #306
Rage of Passion #325
Fit for a King #349
Betrayed by Love #391
‡*Enamored* #420
Reluctant Father #469
Hoodwinked #492
His Girl Friday #528
Hunter #606
Nelson's Brand #618
The Best Is Yet To Come #643
**The Case of the Mesmerizing Boss* #702
**The Case of the Confirmed Bachelor* #715
**The Case of the Missing Secretary* #733
Night of Love #799
Secret Agent Man #829
†*That Burke Man* #913
Man of Ice #1000
The Patient Nurse #1099
†*Beloved* #1189
‡*The Winter Soldier* #1351
†*A Man of Means* #1429
†*Man in Control* #1537

Silhouette Special Edition

Heather's Song #33
The Australian #239
Maggie's Dad #991
†*Matt Caldwell: Texas Tycoon* #1297
‡*The Last Mercenary* #1417

‡*Soldiers of Fortune*
†*Long, Tall Texans*
**Most Wanted Series*

Dear Reader,

As I write this letter, I celebrate another wonderful year at Silhouette Books.

I went to the Romance Writers of America convention in New York City in July of 2003 and was privileged to meet so many of you, my terrific readers. I also enjoyed meeting other authors and making new friends. I had some wonderful meals with my editors at Silhouette, Harlequin and MIRA Books.

I got to tour Harlequin's new Manhattan office, have tea at the Plaza Hotel with a contest winner from Savannah and had supper with my editors, my friend Ann and my son Blayne at the Bull and Bear Restaurant. I went to the Black and White Ball at the Waldorf Astoria Hotel wearing a ball gown and an orchid. Our Harlequin Enterprises President and CEO, Donna M. Hayes, our Vice President of Editorial, Isabel Swift, and my own editor, Tara Gavin—also the Editorial Director in the New York office—presented me with a Tiffany silver heart necklace to mark my one hundred books for the company. I attended the RWA luncheon, where I got another wonderful surprise with two bestseller awards (one for *Desperado* and one for *Lionhearted*) by the wonderful and supportive people at Waldenbooks.

What a trip! I will never forget the experiences or the joy of being with so many nice people.

As I enter my twenty-third year as a Silhouette author, I must tell you that the best part of my job is the people I work with. When I had appendicitis in Chicago in 2001, Isabel Swift and Tara Gavin stayed in the emergency room with me all night—along with my best friend, Ann—and didn't leave until I was out of surgery. To do that, they sacrificed a wonderful meal and some important business activities where they were needed. I know of no better description of true friendship than that; I know of no better job on earth when I do it with people like that.

I wish all of you my very best. Thank you for your years of loyalty and friendship. You are the reason I do the job.

Love to all,

Diana Palmer

Chapter One

Libby Collins couldn't figure out why her stepmother, Janet, had called a real estate agent out to the house. Her father had only been dead for a few weeks. The funeral was so fresh in her mind that she cried herself to sleep at night. Her brother, Curt, was equally devastated. Riddle Collins had been a strong, happy, intelligent man who'd never had a serious illness. He had no history of heart trouble. So his death of a massive heart attack had been a real shock. In fact, the Collinses' nearest neighbor, rancher Jordan Powell, said it was suspicious. But then, Jordan thought everything was suspicious. He thought the government was building cloned soldiers in some underground lab.

Libby ran a small hand through her wavy black hair, her light-green eyes scanning the horizon for a sight of her brother. But Curt was probably up to his ears in watching over the births of early spring cattle, far in the northern pasture of the Powell ranch. It was just barely April and the heifers, the two-year-old first-time mothers, were beginning to drop their calves right on schedule. There was little hope that Curt would show up before the real estate agent left.

Around the corner of the house, Libby heard the real estate agent speaking. She moved closer, careful to keep out of sight, to see what was going on. Her father had loved his small ranch, as his children did. It had been in their family almost as long as Jordan Powell's family had owned the Bar P.

"How long will it take to find a buyer?" Janet was asking.

"I can't really say, Mrs. Collins," the man replied. "But Jacobsville is growing by leaps and bounds. There are plenty of new families looking for reasonable housing. I think a subdivision here would be perfectly situated and I can guarantee you that any developer would pay top dollar for it."

Subdivision?! Surely she must be hearing things!

But Janet's next statement put an end to any such suspicion. "I want to sell it as soon as possible," Janet continued firmly. "I have the insurance money in hand. As soon as this sale is made, I'm moving out of the country."

Another shattering revelation! Why was her stepmother in such a hurry? Her husband of barely nine months had just died, for heaven's sake!

"I'll do what I can, Mrs. Collins," the real estate agent assured her. "But you must understand that the housing market is depressed right now and I can't guarantee a sale—as much as I'd like to."

"Very well," Janet said curtly. "But keep me informed of your progress, please."

"Certainly."

Libby ran for it, careful not to let herself be seen. Her heart was beating her half to death. She'd wondered at Janet's lack of emotion when her father died. Now her mind was forming unpleasant associations.

She stood in the shadows of the front porch until she

heard the real estate agent drive away. Janet left immediately thereafter in her Mercedes.

Libby's mind was whirling. She needed help. Fortunately, she knew exactly where to go to get it.

She walked down the road toward Jordan Powell's big Spanish-style ranch house. The only transportation Libby had was a pickup truck, which was in the shop today having a water pump replaced. It was a long walk to the Powell ranch, but Libby needed fortifying to tackle her stepmother. Jordan was just the person to put steel in her backbone.

It took ten minutes to walk to the paved driveway that led through white fences to the ranch house. But it took another ten minutes to walk from the end of the driveway to the house. On either side of the fence were dark red-coated Santa Gertrudis cattle, purebred seed stock, which were the only cattle Jordan kept. One of his bulls was worth over a million dollars. He had a whole separate division that involved artificial insemination and the care of a special unit where sperm were kept. Libby had been fascinated to know that a single straw of bull semen could sell for a thousand dollars, or much more if it came from a prize bull who was dead. Jordan sold those straws to cattle ranchers all over the world. He frequently had visitors from other countries who came to tour his mammoth cattle operation. Like the Tremayne brothers, Cy Parks, and a number of other local ranchers, he was heavily into organic ranching. He used no hormones or dangerous pesticides or unnecessary antibiotics on his seed stock, even though they were never sold for beef. The herd sires he kept on the ranch lived in a huge breeding barn—as luxurious as a modern hotel—that was on property just adjacent to the Collinses' land. It was so close that they could hear the bulls bellowing from time to time.

Jordan was a local success story, the sort men liked to tell their young sons about. He started out as a cowboy long before he ever had cattle of his own. He'd grown up the only child of a former debutante and a hobby farmer.

His father had married the only child of wealthy parents, who cut her off immediately when she announced her marriage. They left her only the property that Jordan now owned. His father's drinking cost him almost everything. When he wasn't drinking, he made a modest living with a few head of cattle, but after the sudden death of Jordan's mother, he withdrew from the world. Jordan was left with a hard decision to make. He took a job as a ranch hand on Duke Wright's palatial ranch and in his free time he went the rounds of the professional rodeo circuit. He was a champion bull rider, with the belt buckles and the cash to prove it.

But instead of spending that cash on good times, he'd paid off the mortgage that his father had taken on the ranch. Over the years he'd added a purebred Santa Gertrudis bull and a barn, followed by purebred heifers. He'd studied genetics with the help of a nearby retired rancher and he'd learned how to buy straws of bull semen and have his heifers artificially inseminated. His breeding program gave him the opportunity to enter his progeny in competition, which he did. Awards starting coming his way and so did stud fees for his bull. It had been a long road to prosperity, but he'd managed it, despite having to cope with an alcoholic father who eventually got behind the wheel of a truck and plowed it into a telephone pole. Jordan was left alone in the world. Well, except for women. He sure seemed to have plenty of those, to hear her brother Curt talk.

Libby loved the big dusty-yellow adobe ranch house Jordan had built two years ago, with its graceful arches and black wrought-iron grillwork. There was a big fountain in the front courtyard, where Jordan kept goldfish and huge koi that came right up out of the water to look at visitors. It even had a pond heater, to keep the fish alive all winter. It was a dream of a place. It would have been just right for a family. But everybody said that Jordan Powell would never get married. He liked his freedom too much.

She went up to the front door and rang the doorbell. She

knew how she must look in her mud-stained jeans and
faded T-shirt, her boots caked in mud, like her denim
jacket. She'd been helping the lone part-time worker on
their small property pull a calf. It was a dirty business,
something her pristine stepmother would never have done.
Libby still missed her father. His unexpected death had
been a horrible blow to Curt and Libby, who were only
just getting used to Riddle Collins's new wife.

No sooner was Riddle buried than Janet fought to get
her hands on the quarter-of-a-million-dollar insurance policy he'd left behind, of which she alone was listed as beneficiary. She'd started spending money the day the check
had arrived, with no thought for unpaid bills and Riddle's
children. They were healthy and able to work, she reasoned.
Besides, they had a roof over their heads. Temporarily, at
least. Janet's long talk with the real estate agent today was
disquieting. Riddle's new will, which his children knew
nothing about, had given Janet complete and sole ownership of the house as well as Riddle's comfortable but not
excessive savings account. Or so Janet said. Curt was furious. Libby hadn't said anything. She missed her father so
much. She felt as if she were still walking around in a daze
and it was almost March. A windy, cold almost-March, at
that, she thought, feeling the chill.

She was frowning when the door opened. She jumped
involuntarily when instead of the maid, Jordan Powell himself opened it.

"What the hell do you want?" he asked coldly. "Your
brother's not here. He's supervising some new fencing up
on the north property.

"Well?" he asked impatiently when she didn't speak
immediately. "I've got things to do and I'm late already!"

He was so dashing, she thought privately. He was thirty-
two, very tall, lean and muscular, with liquid black eyes
and dark, wavy hair. He had a strong, masculine face that
was dark from exposure to the sun and big ears and big
feet. But he was handsome. Too handsome.

"Are you mute?" he persisted, scowling.

She shook her head, sighing. "I'm just speechless. You really are a dish, Jordan," she drawled.

"Will you please tell me what you want?" he grumbled. "And if it's a date, you can go right back home. I don't like being chased by women. I know you can't keep your eyes off me, but that's no excuse to come sashaying up to my front door looking for attention."

"Fat chance," she drawled, her green eyes twinkling up at him. "If I want a man, I'll try someone accessible, like a movie star or a billionaire...."

"I said I'm in a hurry," he prompted.

"Okay. If you don't want to talk to me..." she began.

He let out an impatient sigh. "Come in, then," he muttered, looking past her. "Hurry, before you get trampled by the other hopeful women chasing me."

"That would be a short list," she told him as she went in and waited until he closed the door behind him. "You're famous for your bad manners. You aren't even housebroken."

"I beg your pardon?" he said curtly.

She grinned at him. "Your boots are full of red mud and so's that fabulously expensive wool rug you brought back from Morocco," she pointed out. "Amie's going to kill you when she sees that."

"My aunt only lives here when she hasn't got someplace else to go," he pointed out.

"Translated, that means that she's in hiding. Why are you mad at her *this* time?" she asked.

He gave her a long-suffering stare and sighed. "Well, she wanted to redo my bedroom. Put yellow curtains at the windows. With ruffles." He spat out the word. "She thinks it's too depressing because I like dark wood and beige curtains."

She lifted both eyebrows over laughing eyes. "You could paint the room red...."

He glared down at her. "I said women chased me, not that I brought them home in buckets," he replied.

"My mistake. Who was it last week, Senator Merrill's daughter, and before her, the current Miss Jacobs County…?"

"That wasn't my fault," he said haughtily. "She stood in the middle of the parking lot at that new Japanese place and refused to move unless I let her come home with me." Then he grinned.

She shook her head. "You're impossible."

"Come on, come on, what do you want?" He looked at his watch. "I've got to meet your brother at the old line cabin in thirty minutes to help look over those pregnant heifers." He lifted an eyebrow and his eyes began to shimmer. They ran up and down her slender figure. "Maybe I could do you justice in fifteen minutes…."

She struck a pose. "Nobody's sticking me in between roundup and supper," she informed him. "Besides, I'm abstaining indefinitely."

He put a hand over his heart. "As God is my witness, I never asked your brother to tell you that Bill Paine had a social disease…"

"I am not sweet on Bill Paine!" she retorted.

"You were going to Houston with him to a concert that wasn't being given that night and I knew that Bill had an apartment and a bad reputation with women," he replied with clenched lips. "So I just happened to mention to one of my cowhands, who was standing beside your brother, that Bill Paine had a social disease."

She was aghast, just standing there gaping at his insolence. Curt had been very angry about her accepting a date with rich, blond Bill, who was far above them in social rank. Bill had been a client of Blake Kemp's, where he noticed Libby and started flirting with her. After Curt had told her what he overheard about Bill, she'd cancelled the date. She was glad she did. Later she'd learned that Bill had made a bet with one of his pals that he could get Libby any time he wanted her, despite her standoffish pose.

"Of course, I don't have any social diseases," Jordan said, his deep voice dropping an octave. He checked his watch again. "Now it's down to ten minutes, if we hurry."

She threw up her hands. "Listen, I can't possibly be seduced today, I've got to go to the grocery store. What I came to tell you is that Janet's selling the property to a developer. He wants to put a subdivision on it," she added miserably.

"A what?" he exploded. "A subdivision? Next door to my breeding barn?!" His eyes began to burn. "Like hell she will!"

"Great. You want to stop her, too. Do you have some strong rope?"

"This is serious," he replied gravely. "What the hell is she doing, selling your home out from under you? Surely Riddle didn't leave her the works! What about you and Curt?"

"She says we're young and can support ourselves," she said, fighting back frustration and fury.

He didn't say anything. His silence was as eloquent as shouting. "She's not evicting you. You go talk to Kemp."

"I work for Mr. Kemp," she reminded him.

He frowned. "Which begs the question, why aren't you at work?"

She sighed. "Mr. Kemp's gone to a bar association conference in Florida," she explained. "He said I could have two vacation days while he's gone, since Mabel and Violet were going to be there in case the attorney covering his practice needed anything." She glowered at him. "I don't get much time off."

"Indeed you don't," he agreed. "Blake Kemp is a busy attorney, for a town the size of Jacobsville. You do a lot of legwork for him, don't you?"

She nodded. "It's part of a paralegal's job. I've learned a lot."

"Enough to tempt you to go to law school?"

She laughed. "No. Not that much. A history degree is enough, not to mention the paralegal training. I've had all the education I want." She frowned thoughtfully. "You know, I did think about teaching adult education classes at night…."

"Your father was well-to-do," he pointed out. "He had coin collections worth half a million, didn't he?"

"We thought so, but we couldn't find them. I suppose he sold them to buy that Mercedes Janet is driving," she said somberly.

"He loved you and Curt."

She had to fight tears. "He wrote a new will just after he married her, leaving everything to her," she said simply. "She said she had it all in his safe-deposit box, along with the passbook to his big savings account, which her name was on as well as his. The way it was set up, that account belonged to her, so there was no legal problem with it," she had to admit. "Daddy didn't leave us a penny."

"There's something fishy going on here," he said, thinking out loud.

"It sounds like it, I guess. But Daddy gave everything to her. That was his decision to make, not ours. He was crazy about her."

Jordan looked murderous. "Has the will gone through probate yet?"

She shook her head. "She said she's given it to an attorney. It's pending."

"You know the law, even better than I do. This isn't right. You should get a lawyer," he repeated. "Get Kemp, in fact, and have him investigate her. There's something not right about this, Libby. Your father was the healthiest man I ever knew. He never had any symptoms of heart trouble."

"Well, I thought that, too, and so did Curt." She sighed, glancing down at the elegant blue and rose carpet, and her eyes grew misty. "He was really crazy about her, though.

Maybe he just didn't think we'd need much. I know he loved us…." She choked back a sob. It was still fresh, the grief.

Jordan sighed and pulled her close against his tall, powerful body. His arms were warm and comforting as they enfolded her. "Why don't you just cry, Libby?" he asked gently. "It does help."

She sniffed into his shoulder. It smelled nice. His shirt had a pleasant detergent smell to it. "Do you ever cry?"

"Bite your tongue, woman," he said at her temple. "What would happen to the ranch if I sat down and bawled every time something went wrong? Tears won't come out of Persian carpet, you just ask my aunt!"

She laughed softly, even through the tears. He was a comforting sort of man and it was surprising, because he had a quick temper and an arrogance that put most people's backs up at first meeting.

"So that's why you yell at your cowboys? So you won't cry?"

"Works for me," he chuckled. He patted her shoulder. "Feel better?"

She nodded, smiling through tears. She wiped them away with a paper towel she'd tucked into her jeans. "Thanks."

"What are prospective lovers for?" he asked, smiling wickedly, and laughing out loud when she flushed.

"You stop corrupting me, you bad influence!"

"I said nothing corrupting, I just gave advance notice of bad intentions." He laughed at her expression. "At least it stopped the cascading waterfalls," he added, tongue in cheek, as he glanced at the tear tracks down her cheeks.

"Those weren't tears," she mumbled. "It was dew." She held up a hand. "I feel it falling again!"

"Talk to Kemp," he reiterated, not adding that he was going to do the same. "If she's got a new will and a codicil, signed, make her prove it. Don't let her shove you off your own land without a fight."

"I guess I could ask to see it," she agreed. Then she winced. "I hate arguments. I hate fights."

"I'll remember that the next time you come chasing after me," he promised.

She shook her head impotently, turning to go.

"Hey."

She glanced at him over her shoulder.

"Let me know what you find out," he said. "I'm in this, too. I can't manage a subdivision right near my barn. I can't have a lot of commotion around those beautiful Santa Gerts, it stresses them too much. It would cost a fortune to tear down that barn and stick it closer to the house. A lawsuit would be cheaper."

"There's an idea," she said brightly. "Take her to court."

"For what, trying to sell property? That's rich."

"Just trying to help us both out," she said.

He glanced at his watch again. "Five minutes left and even I'm not that good," he added. "Pity. If you hadn't kept running your mouth, by now we could have…"

"You hush, Jordan Powell!" she shot at him. "Honestly, of all the blatant, arrogant, sex-crazed ranchers in Texas…!"

She was still mumbling as she went out the door. But when she was out of sight, she grinned. He was a tonic.

That night, Janet didn't say a word about any real estate deals. She ate a light supper that Libby had prepared, as usual without any compliments about it.

"When are you going back to work?" she asked Libby irritably, her dyed blond hair in an expensive hairdo, her trendy silk shell and embroidered jeans marking her new wealth. "It can't be good for you to lie around here all day."

Curt, who was almost the mirror image of his sister, except for his height and powerful frame, glared at the woman. "Excuse me, since when did you do any housework or cooking around here? Libby's done both since she turned thirteen!''

''Don't you speak to me that way,'' Janet said haughtily. ''I can throw you out any time I like. I own everything!''

''You don't own the property until that will goes through probate,'' Libby replied sweetly, shocked at her own boldness. She'd never talked that way to the woman before. ''You can produce it, I hope, because you're going to have to. You don't get the property yet. Maybe not even later, if everything isn't in perfect order.''

''You've been talking to that rancher again, haven't you?'' Janet demanded. ''That damned Powell man! He's so suspicious about everything! Your father had a heart attack. He's dead. He left everything to me. What else do you want?'' she raged, standing.

Libby stood, too, her face flushed. ''Proof. I want proof. And you'd better have it before you start making any deals with developers about selling Daddy's land!''

Janet started. ''De...developers?''

''I heard you this afternoon with that real estate agent,'' Libby said, with an apologetic glance at her brother, who looked shocked. She hadn't told him. ''You're trying to sell our ranch and Daddy hasn't even been dead a month!''

Curt stood up. He looked even more formidable than Libby. ''Before you make any attempt to sell this land, you're going to need a lawyer, Janet,'' he said in that slow, cold drawl that made cowhands move faster.

''How are you going to afford one, Curt, dear?'' she asked sarcastically. ''You just work for wages.''

''Oh, Jordan will loan us the money,'' Libby said confidently.

Janet's haughty expression fluttered. She threw down her napkin. ''You need cooking lessons,'' she said spitefully. ''This food is terrible! I've got to make some phone calls.''

She stormed out of the room.

Libby and Curt sat back down, both angry. Libby explained about the real estate agent's visit and what she'd overheard. Curt had only just come in when Libby had put the spaghetti and garlic bread on the table. It was Curt's favorite food and his sister made it very well, he thought, despite Janet's snippy comment.

"She's not selling this place while there's a breath left in my body," he told his sister. "Anyway, she can't do that until the will is probated. And she'd better have a legitimate will."

"Jordan said we needed to get Mr. Kemp to take a look at it," she said. "And I think we're going to need a handwriting expert to take a look, too."

He nodded.

"But what are we going to do about money to file suit?" she asked. "I was bluffing about Jordan loaning us the money. I don't know if he would."

"He's not going to want a subdivision on his doorstep, I'll tell you that," Curt said. "I'll talk to him."

"I already did," she said, surprising him. "He thinks there's something fishy going on, too."

"You can't get much past Jordan," he agreed. "I've been working myself to death trying not to think about losing Dad. I should have paid more attention to what was going on here."

"I've been grieving, too." She sighed and folded her small hands on the tablecloth. "Isn't it amazing how snippy she is, now that Daddy's not here? She was all over us like poison ivy before he died."

"She married him for what he had, Libby," he said bitterly.

"She seemed to love him...."

"She came on to me the night they came back from that Cancun honeymoon," he said bitterly.

Libby whistled. Her brother was a very attractive man. Their father, a sweet and charming man, had been overweight and balding. She could understand why Janet might have preferred Curt to his father.

"I slapped her down hard and Dad never knew." He

shook his head. "How could he marry something like that?"

"He was flattered by all the attention she gave him, I guess," Libby said miserably. "And now here we are. I'll bet she sweet-talked him into changing that will. He would have done anything for her, you know that—he was crazy in love with her. He might have actually written us out of it, Curt. We have to accept that."

"Not until they can prove to me that it wasn't forged," he said stubbornly. "I'm not giving up our inheritance without a fight. Neither are you," he asserted.

She sighed. "Okay, big brother. What do you want to do?"

"When do you go back to work?"

"Monday. Mr. Kemp's out of town."

"Okay. Monday, you make an appointment for both of us to sit down with him and hash this out."

She felt better already. "Okay," she said brightly. "I'll do that very thing. Maybe we do have a chance of keeping Daddy's ranch."

He nodded. "There's always hope." He leaned back in his chair. "So you went to see Jordan." He smiled indulgently. "I can remember a time not so long ago when you ran and hid from him."

"He always seemed to be yelling at somebody," she recalled. "I was intimidated by him. Especially when I graduated from high school. I had a sort of crush on him. I was scared to death he'd notice. Not that he was ever around here that much," she added, laughing. "He and Daddy had a fight a week over water rights."

"Dad usually lost, too," Curt recalled. He studied his sister with affection. "You know, I thought maybe Jordan was sweet on you himself—he's only eight years older than you."

"He's never been sweet on me!" she flashed at him, blushing furiously. "He's hardly even smiled at me, in all the years we've lived here, until the past few months! If anything, he usually treats me like a contagious virus!''

Curt only smiled. He looked very much like her, with the same dark wavy hair and the same green eyes. ''He picks at you. Teases you. Makes you laugh. You do the same thing to him. People besides me have noticed. He bristles if anyone says anything unkind about you.''

Her eyes widened. ''Who's been saying unkind things about me?'' she asked.

''That assistant store manager over at Lord's Department Store.''

''Oh. Sherry King.'' She leaned back in her chair. ''She can't help it, you know. She was crazy about Duke Wright and he wanted to take me to the Cattleman's Ball. I wouldn't go and he didn't ask anybody else. I feel sorry for her.''

''Duke's not your sort of man,'' he replied. ''He's a mixer. Nobody in Jacobsville has been in more brawls,'' he said, pausing. ''Well, maybe Leo Hart has.''

''Leo Hart got married, he won't be brawling out at Shea's Roadhouse and Bar anymore.''

''Duke's not likely to get married again. His wife took their five-year-old son to New York City, where her new job is. He says she doesn't even look after the little boy. She's too busy trying to get a promotion. The child stays with her sister while she jets all over the world closing real estate deals.''

''It's a new world,'' Libby pointed out. ''Women are competing with men for the choice jobs now. They have to move around to get a promotion.''

Curt's eyes narrowed. ''Maybe they should get promotion before they get pregnant,'' he said impatiently.

She shrugged. ''Accidents happen.''

''No child of mine is ever going to be an accident,'' Curt said firmly.

''Nice to be so superior,'' she teased, eyes twinkling. ''Never to make mistakes…''

He swiped at her with a napkin. "You don't even stick your toes in the water, so don't lecture me about drowning."

She chuckled. "I'm sensible, I am," she retorted. "None of this angst for me. I'll just do my routine job and keep my nose out of emotional entanglements."

He studied her curiously. "You go through life avoiding any sort of risk, don't you, honey?" he mused.

She moved one shoulder restlessly. "Daddy and Mama fought all the time, remember?" she said. "I swore I'd never get myself into a fix like that. She told me that she and Daddy were so happy when they first met, when they first married. Then, six months later, she was pregnant with you and they couldn't manage one pleasant meal together without shouting." She shook her head. "That means you can't trust emotions. It's better to use your brain when you think about marrying somebody. Love is...sticky," she concluded. "And it causes insanity, I'm sure of it."

"Why don't you ask Kemp if that's why he's stayed single so long? He's in his middle thirties, isn't he, and never even been engaged."

"Who'd put up with him?" she asked honestly. "Now there's a mixer for you," she said enthusiastically. "He actually *threw* another lawyer out the front door and onto the sidewalk last month. Good thing there was a welcome mat there, it sort of broke the guy's fall."

"What did he want?" Curt asked.

She shook her head. "I have no idea. But I don't expect him to be a repeat client."

Curt chuckled. "I see what you mean."

Libby went to bed early that night, without another word to Janet. She knew that anything she said would be too much. But she did miss her father and she couldn't believe that he wouldn't have mentioned Libby and Curt in his will. He did love them. She knew he did.

She thought about Jordan Powell, too, and about Curt's

remark that he thought Jordan was sweet on her. She tingled all over at the thought. But that wasn't going to happen, she assured herself. Jordan was gorgeous and he could have his pick of pretty women. Libby Collins would be his last resort. The world wasn't ending yet, so she was out of the running.

She rolled over, closed her eyes, and went to sleep.

Chapter Two

Janet wasn't at breakfast the next morning. Her new gold Mercedes was gone and she hadn't left a note. Libby saw it as a bad omen.

The weekend passed with nothing remarkable except for Janet's continued absence. The truck was ready Saturday and Curt picked it up in town, catching a lift with one of Jordan's cowboys. It wasn't as luxurious as a Mercedes, but it had a good engine and it was handy for hauling things like salt blocks and bales of hay. Libby tried to picture hauling hay in Janet's Mercedes and almost went hysterical with laughter.

Libby went back to work at Blake Kemp's office early Monday morning, dropped off by Curt on his way to the feed store for Jordan. She felt as if she hadn't really had a vacation at all.

Violet Hardy, Mr. Kemp's secretary, who was dark-haired, blue-eyed, pretty and somewhat overweight, smiled at her as she came in the door. "Hi! Did you have a nice vacation?"

"I spent it working," Libby confessed. "How did things go here?"

Violet groaned. "Don't even ask."

"That bad, huh?" Libby remarked.

Mabel, the blond grandmother who worked at reception, turned in her chair after transferring a call into Mr. Kemp's office. "Bad isn't the word, Libby," she said in a whisper, glancing down the hall to make sure the doors were all closed. "That lawyer Mr. Kemp got to fill in for him got two cases confused and sent the clients to the wrong court-rooms in different counties."

"Yes," Violet nodded, "and one of them came in here and tried to punch Mr. Kemp."

Libby pursed her lips. "No. Did he have insurance?"

All three women chuckled.

"For an attorney who handles so many assault cases," Violet whispered, "he doesn't practice what he preaches. Mr. Kemp punched the guy back and they wound up out on the street. Our police chief, Cash Grier, broke it up and almost arrested Mr. Kemp."

"What about the other guy? Didn't he start it?" Libby exclaimed.

"The other guy was Duke Wright," Violet confessed, watching Libby color. "And Chief Grier said that instead of blaming Mr. Kemp for handling Mrs. Wright's divorce, he should thank him for not bankrupting Mr. Wright in the process!"

"Then what?" Libby asked.

All three women glanced quickly down the hall.

"Mr. Wright threw a punch at Chief Grier."

"Well, that was smart thinking. Duke's in the hospital, then?" Libby asked facetiously.

"Nope," Violet said, her blue eyes twinkling. "But he was in jail briefly until he made bail." She shook her head. "I don't expect he'll try that twice."

"Crime has fallen about fifty percent since we got Cash Grier as chief," Violet sighed, smiling.

"And Judd Dunn as assistant chief," Libby reminded her.

"Poor Mr. Wright," Mabel said. "He does have the worst luck. Remember that Jack Clark who worked for him, who was convicted of murdering that woman in Victoria? Mr. Wright sure hated the publicity. It came just when he was trying to get custody of his son."

"Mr. Wright would have a lot less trouble if he didn't spend so much time out looking for it," came a deep, gruff voice from behind them.

They all jumped. Blake Kemp was standing just at the entrance to the hallway with a brief in one hand and a coffee cup in the other. He was as much a dish as Jordan Powell. He had wavy dark hair and blue eyes and the most placid, friendly face—until he got in front of a jury. Nobody wanted to be across the courtroom from Kemp when a trial began. There was some yellow and purple discoloration on one high cheekbone, where a fist had apparently landed a blow. Duke Wright, Libby theorized silently.

"Libby, before you do anything else, would you make a pot of coffee, please?" he asked in a long-suffering tone. He impaled a wincing Violet with his pale blue eyes. "I don't give a damn what some study says is best for me, I want caffeine. C-A-F-F-E-I-N-E," he added, spelling it letter by letter for Violet's benefit.

Violet lifted her chin and her own blue eyes glared right back at him. "Mr. Kemp, if you drank less of it, you might not be so bad-tempered. I mean, really, that's the second person you've thrown out of our office in a month! Chief Grier said that was a new city record...."

Kemp's eyes were blazing now, narrow and intent. "Miss Hardy, do you want to still be employed here tomorrow?"

Violet looked as if she was giving that question a lot of deliberation. "But, sir…" she began.

"I like caffeine. I'm not giving it up," Kemp said curtly. "You don't change my routine in this office. Is that clear?"

"But, Mr. Kemp—!" she argued.

"I don't remember suggesting anything so personal to you, Miss Hardy," he shot back, clearly angry. "I could, however," he added, and his cold blue eyes made insinuations about her figure, which was at least two dress sizes beyond what it should have been.

All three women gasped at the outrageous insinuation and then glared at their boss.

Violet flushed and stood up, as angry as he was, but not intimidated one bit by the stare. "My...my father always said that a woman should look like a woman and not a skeleton encased in skin. I may be a little overweight, Mr. Kemp, but at least I'm doing something about it!"

He glanced pointedly at a cake in a box on her desk.

She colored. "I live out near the Hart Ranch. I promised Tess Hart I'd pick that up at the bakery for her before I came to work and drop it by her house when I go home for lunch. It's for a charity tea party this afternoon." She was fuming. "I do not eat cake! Not anymore."

He stared at her until she went red and sat back down. She averted her eyes and went back to work. Her hands on the computer keyboard were trembling.

"You fire me if you want to, Mr. Kemp, but nothing I said to you was as mean as what you were insinuating to me with that look," Violet choked. "I know I weigh too much. You don't have to rub it in. I was only trying to help you."

Mabel and Libby were still glaring at him. He shifted uncomfortably and put the brief down on Violet's desk with a slap. "There are six spelling errors in that. You'll have to redo it. You can buzz me when the coffee's ready," he added shortly. He turned on his heel and took his coffee cup back into his office. As an afterthought, he slammed the door.

"Oh, and like anybody short of a druggist could read those chicken scratches on paper that you call *handwriting!*" Violet muttered, staring daggers after him.

Libby let out the breath she'd been holding and gaped at sweet, biddable Violet, who'd never talked back to Mr. Kemp in the eight months she'd worked for him. So did Mabel.

"Well, it's about time!" Mabel said, laughing delightedly. "Good for you, Violet. It's no good, letting a man walk all over you, no matter how crazy you are about him!"

"Hush!" Violet exclaimed, glancing quickly down the hall. "He'll hear you!"

"He doesn't know," Libby said comfortingly, putting an arm around Violet. "And we'll never tell. I'm proud of you, Violet."

"Me, too," Mabel grinned.

Violet sighed. "I guess he'll fire me. It might not be a bad thing. I spend too much time trying to take care of him and he hates it." Her blue eyes were wistful under their long, thick lashes. "You know, I've lost fifteen pounds," she murmured. "And I'm down a dress size."

"A new diet?" Libby asked absently as she checked her "in" tray.

"A new gym, just for women," Violet confessed with a grin. "I love it!"

Libby looked at the other woman with admiration. "You're really serious about this, aren't you?"

Violet's shoulder moved gently. She was wearing a purple dress with a high collar and lots of frills on the bodice and a very straight skirt that clung to her hips. It was the worst sort of dress for a woman who had a big bust and wide hips, but nobody had the heart to tell Violet. "I had to do something. I mean, look at me! I'm so big!"

"You're not that big. But I think it's great that you're trying so hard, Violet," Libby said gently. "And to keep you on track, Mabel and I are giving up dessert when you eat lunch with us."

"I have to go home and see about Mother most every day at lunchtime," Violet confessed. "She hates that. She said I was wasting my whole life worrying about her, when I should be out having fun. But she's already had two light strokes in the past year since Daddy died. I can't leave her alone.''

"Honey, people like you are why there's a heaven," Mabel murmured softly. "You're one in a million.''

Violet waved her away. "Everybody's got problems," she laughed. "For all we know, Mr. Kemp has much bigger ones than we do. He's such a good person. When Mother had that last stroke, the bad one, he even drove me to the hospital after I got the call.''

"He is a good person," Libby agreed. "But so are you.''

"You'd better make that coffee, I guess," Violet said wistfully. "I really thought I could make it half and half and he wouldn't be able to taste the difference. He's so uptight lately. He's always in a hurry, always under pressure. He drinks caffeine like water and it's so bad for his heart. I know about hearts. My dad died of a heart attack last year. I was just trying to help.''

"It's hard to help a rattlesnake across the road, Violet," Mabel said, tongue-in-cheek.

Libby was curious about the coincidence of Violet's father dying of a heart attack, like her father, such a short time ago. "Violet could find one nice thing to say about a serial killer," Libby agreed affectionately. "Even worse, she could find one nice thing to say about my stepmother.''

"Ouch," Mabel groaned. "Now there's a hard case if I ever saw one." She shook her head. "People in Branntville are still talking about her and old man Darby.''

Libby, who'd just finished filling the coffeepot, started it brewing and turned jerkily. "Excuse me?''

"Didn't I ever tell you?" Mabel asked absently. "Just a sec. Good morning, Kemp Law Offices," she said. "Yes, sir, I'll connect you." She started to push the intercom button when she saw with shock that it was already depressed. The light was on the switch. She and Libby, who'd also seen it, exchanged agonized glances. Quickly, without telling Violet, she pushed it off and then on again. "Mr. Kemp, it's Mrs. Lawson for you on line two." She waited, hung up, and swung her chair around. She didn't dare tell poor Violet that Mr. Kemp had probably heard every single word she'd said about him.

"Your stepmother, Janet," Mabel told Libby, "was working at a nursing home over in Branntville. She sweet-talked an old man who was a patient there into leaving everything he had to her." She shook her head. "They said that Janet didn't even give him a proper funeral. She had him cremated and put in an urn and there was a graveside service. They said she bought a designer suit to wear to it."

Libby was getting cold chills. There were too many similarities there to be a coincidence. Janet had wanted to have Riddle Collins cremated, too, but Curt and Libby had talked to the funeral director and threatened a lawsuit if he complied with Janet's request. They went home and told Janet the same thing and also insisted on a church funeral at the Presbyterian church where Riddle had been a member since childhood. Janet had been furious, but in the end, she reluctantly agreed.

Violet wasn't saying anything, but she had a funny look on her face and she seemed pale. She turned away before the others saw. But Libby's expression was thought-provoking.

"You're thinking something. What?" Mabel asked Libby.

Fortunately, the phone rang again while Libby was deciding if it was wise to share her thoughts.

Violet got up from her desk and went close to Libby. "She wanted to cremate your father, too, didn't she?"

Libby nodded.

"You should go talk to Mr. Kemp."

Libby smiled. "You know, Violet, I think you're right." She hugged the other girl and went back to Mabel. "When he gets off the phone, I need to talk to him."

Mabel grinned. "Now you're talking." She checked the board. "He's free. Just a sec." She pushed a button. "Mr. Kemp, Libby needs to speak to you, if it's convenient."

"Send her in, Mrs. Jones."

"Good luck," Mabel said, crossing her fingers.

Libby grinned back.

"Come in," Kemp said, opening the door for Libby and closing it behind her. "Have a seat. I don't need ESP to know what's on your mind. I had a call from Jordan Powell at home last night."

Her eyebrows arched. "Well, he jumped the gun!"

"He's concerned. Probably with good reason," he added. "I went ahead on my own and had a private detective I know run a check on Janet's background. This isn't the first time she's become a widow."

"I know," Libby said. "Mabel says an elderly man in a nursing home left her everything he had. She had him sent off to be cremated immediately after they got him to the funeral home."

He nodded. "And I understand from Don Hedgely at our funeral home here that she tried to have the same thing done with your father, but you and your brother threatened a lawsuit."

"We did," Libby said. "Daddy didn't believe in cremation. He would have been horrified."

Kemp leaned back in his desk chair and crossed his long legs, with his hands behind his head. He pursed his lips and narrowed his blue eyes, deep in thought. "There's another thing," he said. "Janet was fired from that nursing home for being too friendly with their wealthiest patients. One of whom—the one you know about—was an elderly widower with no children. He died of suspicious causes and left her his estate."

Libby folded her arms. She felt chilled all over now. "Wasn't it enough for her?" she wondered out loud.

"Actually, it took the entire estate to settle his gambling

debts," he murmured. "Apparently, he liked the horses a little too much."

"Then there was our father." She anticipated his next thought.

He shook his head. "That was after Mr. Hardy in San Antonio."

Libby actually gasped. It couldn't be!

Kemp leaned forward quickly. "Do you think Violet is happy having to live in a rented firetrap with her invalid mother? Her parents were wealthy. But a waitress at Mr. Hardy's favorite restaurant apparently began a hot affair with him and talked him into making her a loan of a quarter of a million dollars to save her parents from bankruptcy and her father from suicide. He gave her a check and had a heart attack before he could stop payment on it—which he planned to do. He told his wife and begged forgiveness of her and his daughter before he died." His eyes narrowed. "He died shortly after he was seen with a pretty blonde at a San Antonio motel downtown."

"You think it was Janet? That it wasn't a heart attack at all—that she killed him?"

"I think there are too many coincidences for comfort in her past," Kemp said flatly. "But the one eyewitness who saw her with Hardy at that motel was unable to pick her out of a lineup. She'd had her hair color changed just the day before the lineup. She remained a brunette for about a week and then changed back to blond."

Libby's face tightened. "She might have killed my father," she bit off.

"That is a possibility," Kemp agreed. "It's early days yet, Libby. I can't promise you anything. But if she's guilty and I can get her on a witness stand, in a court of law, I can break her," he said with frightening confidence. "She'll tell me everything she knows."

She swallowed. "I don't want her to get away with it," she began. "But Curt and I work for wages…"

He flapped his hand in her direction. "Every lawyer

takes a pro bono case occasionally. I haven't done it in months. You and Curt can be my public service for the year," he added, and he actually smiled. It made him look younger, much less dangerous than he really was.

"I don't know what to say," she said, shaking her head in disbelief.

He leaned forward. "Say you'll be careful," he replied. "I can't find any suspicion that she ever helped a young person have a heart attack, but I don't doubt for a minute that she knows how. I'm working with Micah Steele on that aspect of it. There isn't much he doesn't know about the darker side of medicine, even if he is a doctor. And what he doesn't know about black ops and untimely death, Cash Grier does."

"I thought Daddy died of a heart condition nobody knew he had." She took a deep breath. "When I tell Curt, he'll go crazy."

"Let me tell him," Kemp said quietly. "It will be easier."

"Okay."

"Meanwhile, you have to go back home and pretend that nothing's wrong, that your stepmother is innocent of any foul play. That's imperative. If you give her a reason to think she's being suspected of anything, she'll bolt, and we may never find her."

"We'd get our place back without a fight," Libby commented wistfully.

"And a woman who may have murdered your father, among others, would go free," Kemp replied. "Is that really what you want?"

Libby shook her head. "Of course not. I'll do whatever you say."

"We'll be working in the background. The most important thing is to keep the pressure on, a little at a time, so that she doesn't get suspicious. Tell her you've spoken to an attorney about the will, but nothing more."

"Okay," she agreed.

He got up. "And don't tell Violet I said anything to you about her father," he added. His broad shoulders moved restlessly under his expensive beige suit, as if he were carrying some difficult burden. "She's…sensitive."

What a surprising comment from such an insensitive man, she thought, but she didn't dare say it. She only smiled. "Certainly."

She was reaching for the doorknob when he called her back. "Yes, sir?"

"When you make another pot of coffee," he said hesitantly, "I guess we could use some of that half and half."

Her dropped jaw told its own story.

"She means well," he said abruptly, and turned back to his desk. "But for now, I want it strong and black and straight up. Call me when it's made and I'll bring my cup."

"It should be ready right now," she faltered. Even in modern times, few bosses went to get their own coffee. But Mr. Kemp was something of a puzzle. Perhaps, Libby thought wickedly as she followed him down the hall, even to himself.

He glanced at Violet strangely, but he didn't make any more comments. Violet sat with her eyes glued to her computer screen until he poured his coffee and went back to his office.

Libby wanted so badly to say something to her, but she didn't know what. In the end, she just smiled and made a list of the legal precedents she would have to look up for Mr. Kemp at the law library in the county courthouse. Thank God, she thought, for computers.

She was on her way home in the pickup truck after a long day when she saw Jordan on horseback, watching several men drive the pregnant heifers into pastures close to the barn. He had a lot of money invested in those purebred calves and he wasn't risking them to predators or difficult births. He looked so good on horseback, she thought dreamily. He was arrow-straight and his head, covered by that wide-brimmed creamy Stetson he favored, was tilted in a way that was particularly his. She could have picked him out of any crowd at a distance just by the way he carried himself.

He turned his head when he heard the truck coming down the long dirt road and he motioned Libby over to the side.

She parked the truck, cut off the engine, and stood on the running board to talk to him over the top of the old vehicle. "I wish I had a camera," she called. "Mama Powell, protecting his babies…"

"You watch it!" he retorted, shaking a finger at her.

She laughed. "What are you going to do, jump the fence and run me down?"

"Poor old George here couldn't jump a fence. He's twenty-four," he added, patting the old horse's withers. "He hates his corral. I thought I'd give him a change of scenery, since I wasn't going far."

"Everything gets old, I guess. Most everything, anyway," she added with a faraway, wistful look in her eyes. She had an elderly horse of her own, that she might yet have to give away because it was hard to feed and keep him on her salary.

He dismounted and left George's reins on the ground to jump the fence and talk to her. "Did you see Kemp?" he asked.

"Yes. He said you phoned him."

"I asked a few questions and got some uncomfortable answers," he said, coming around the truck to stand beside her. His big lean hands went to her waist and he lifted her down close to him. Too close. She could smell his shaving lotion and feel the heat off his body under the Western cut long-sleeved shirt. In her simple, jacketed suit, she felt overly dressed.

"You don't look too bad when you fix up," he commented, approving her light makeup and the gray suit that made her eyes look greener than they were.

"You don't look too bad when you don't," she replied. "What uncomfortable answers are you getting?"

His eyes were solemn. "I think you can guess. I don't like the idea of you and Curt alone in that house with her."

"We have a shotgun somewhere. I'll make a point of buying some shells for it."

He shook her by the waist gently. "I'm not teasing. Can you lock your bedroom door? Can Curt?"

"It's an old house, Jordan," she faltered. "None of the bedroom doors have locks."

"Tell Curt I said to get bolts and put them on. Do it when she's not home. In the meantime, put a chair under the doorknob."

"But why?" she asked uncertainly.

He drew a long breath. His eyes went to her soft bow of a mouth and he studied it for several seconds before he spoke. "There's one very simple way to cause a heart attack. You can do it with a hypodermic syringe filled with nothing but air."

She couldn't speak for a moment. "Could they…tell that if they did an autopsy on my father?"

"I'm not a forensic specialist, despite the fact that there are half a dozen shows on TV that can teach you how to think you are. I'll ask somebody who knows," he added.

She hated the thought of disinterring her father. But it would be terrible if he'd met with foul play and it never came out.

He tilted her face up to his narrow dark eyes. "You're worrying. Don't. I'm as close as your phone, night or day."

She smiled gently. "Thanks, Jordan."

His thumbs moved on her waist while he looked down at her. His face hardened. His eyes were suddenly on her soft mouth, with real hunger.

The world stopped. It seemed like that. She met his searching gaze and couldn't breathe. Her body felt achy. Hungry. Feverish. She swallowed, hoping it didn't show.

"If you play your cards right, I might let you kiss me," he murmured.

Her heart skipped. "Excuse me?"

One big shoulder lifted and fell. "Where else are you going to get any practical experience?" he asked. "Duke Wright is a candidate for the local nursing home, after all…"

"He's thirty-six!" she exclaimed. "That isn't old!"

"I'm thirty-two," he pointed out. "I have all my own teeth." He grinned to display them. "And I can still outrun at least two of my horses."

"That's an incentive to kiss you?" she asked blankly.

"Think of the advantages if you kiss me during a stampede," he pointed out.

She laughed. He was a case. Her eyes adored him. "I'll keep you in mind," she promised. "But you mustn't get your hopes up. This town is full of lonely bachelors who can't get women to kiss them. You'll have to take a number and wait."

"Wait until what?" he asked, tweaking her waist with his thumbs.

"I don't know. Christmas? I could kiss you as part of your present."

His eyebrows arched. "What's the other part?"

"It's not Christmas. Listen, I have to get home and make supper."

"I'll send Curt on down," he said.

She was seeing a new pattern. "To make sure I'm not left alone with Janet, is that right?"

"For my peace of mind," he corrected. "I've gotten… used to you," he added slowly. "As a neighbor," he added deliberately. "Think how hard it would be to break in another one, at my age."

"You just said you weren't old," she reminded him.

"Maybe I am, just a little," he confessed. He drew her up until she was standing completely against him, so close that she could feel the hard press of his muscular legs

against her own. "Come on," he taunted, bending his head
with a mischievous little smile. "You know you're dying
to kiss me."

"I am?" she whispered dreamily as she studied the long,
wide, firm curve of his lips.

"Desperately."

She felt his nose brushing against hers. Somewhere, a
horse was neighing. A jet flew over. The wind ruffled
leaves in a small tree nearby. She was deaf to any sound
other than the throb of her own heartbeat. There was nothing in the world except Jordan's mouth, a scant inch from
her own. He'd never kissed her. She wanted him to. She
ached for him to.

His hands tightened on her waist, lifting her closer.
"Come on, chicken. Give it all you've got."

Her hands were flat against his chest, feeling the warm
muscles under his cotton shirt. She tasted his breath. Her
arms slid up to his shoulders. He had her hypnotized. She
wanted nothing more than to drown in him.

"That's it," he whispered.

She closed her eyes and lifted up on her tiptoes as she
felt the slow, soft press of her own lips against his for the
first time.

Her knees were weak. She didn't think they were going
to support her. And still Jordan didn't move, didn't re-
spond.

Frustrated, she tried to lift up higher, her arms circled
his neck and pulled, trying to make his mouth firm and
deepen above hers. But she couldn't budge him.

"Oh, you arro…!"

It was the opening he'd been waiting for. His mouth
crushed down against her open lips and his arms contracted
hungrily. Libby moaned sharply at the rush of sensation it
caused in her body. It had never been like this in her life.
She was burning alive. She ached. She longed. She couldn't
get close enough….

"Hey, Jordan!"

The distant shout broke the spell. Jordan jerked his head around to see one of his men waving a wide-brimmed hat and gesturing toward a pickup truck that was driving right out into the pasture where Jordan was putting those pregnant heifers.

"It's the feed supplement I ordered," he murmured, letting her go slowly. "Damn his timing."

He didn't smile when he said that. She couldn't manage even a word.

He touched her softly swollen mouth with his fingertips. "Maybe you could take me on a date and we could get lost on some deserted country road," he suggested.

She took a breath and shook her head to clear it. "I do not seduce men in parked cars," she pointed out.

He snapped his fingers. "Damn!"

"He's waving at you again," she noted, looking over his shoulder.

"All right, I'll go to work. But I'll send Curt on home." He touched her cheek. "Be careful, okay?"

She managed a weak smile. "Okay."

He turned and vaulted the fence, mounting George with the ease of years of practice as a horseman. "See you."

She nodded and watched him ride away. Her life had just changed course, in the most unexpected way.

Chapter Three

But all Jordan's worry—and Libby's unease—was for nothing. When she got home, Janet's Mercedes was gone. There was a terse little note on the hall table that read, *Gone to Houston shopping, back tomorrow.*

Even as she was reading it, Curt came in the back door, bareheaded and sweaty.

"She's gone?" he asked.

She nodded. "Left a note. She's gone to Houston and won't be back until tomorrow."

"Great. It'll give me time to put locks on the bedroom doors," he said.

She sighed. "Jordan's been talking to you, hasn't he?" she asked.

"Yes, and he's been kissing you, apparently," he murmured, grinning. "Old Harry had to yell himself hoarse to get Jordan's attention when they brought those feed supplements out."

She flushed. She couldn't think of a single defense. But she hadn't heard Harry yelling, except one time. No wonder people were talking.

"Interested in you, is he?" Curt asked softly.

"He wanted me to ask him out on a date and get him lost on a dirt road," she said.

"And you said...?"

She moved restively. "I said that I didn't seduce men in parked cars on deserted roads, of course," she assured him.

He looked solemn. "Sis, we've never really talked about Jordan...."

"And we really don't need to, now," she interrupted. "I'm a big girl and I know all about Jordan. He's only teasing. I'm older and he's doing it in a different way, that's all."

Curt wasn't smiling. "He isn't."

She cleared her throat. "Well, it doesn't matter. He's not a marrying man and I'm not a frivolous woman. Besides, his tastes run to beauty queens and state senators' daughters."

He hesitated.

She smiled before he could say anything else. "Let it drop. We've got enough on our minds now without adding more to them. Let's rush to the hardware store and buy locks before she gets back."

He shrugged and let it go. There would be another time to discuss Jordan Powell.

When Libby got home from work Tuesday evening she was still reeling from the shocking news that a fed-up Violet had quit her job and gone to work for Dick Wright. Blake Kemp had *not* taken the news well. Her mood lifted when she found Jordan's big burgundy double-cabbed pickup truck sitting in her front yard. He was sitting on the side of the truck bed, whittling a piece of wood with a pocket knife, his broad-brimmed hat pushed way back on his head. He looked up at her approach and jumped down to meet her.

"You're late," he complained.

She got out of her car, grabbing her purse on the way. "I had to stay late and type up some notes for Mr. Kemp."

He scowled. "That's Violet's job."

"Violet's leaving," she said on a sigh. "She's going to work for Duke Wright."

"But she's crazy for Kemp, isn't she?" Jordan wondered.

She scowled at him. "You aren't supposed to know that," she pointed out.

"Everybody knows that." He looked around the yard. "Janet hasn't shown up. Curt said she'd gone to Houston."

"That's what the note said," she agreed, walking beside him to the front porch. "Curt put the locks on last night."

"I know. I asked him."

She unlocked the door and pushed it open. "Want some coffee?"

"I'd love some. Eggs? Bacon? Cinnamon toast?" he added.

"Oh, I see," she mused with a grin. "Amie's gone and you're starving, huh?"

He shrugged nonchalantly. "She didn't have to leave. I only yelled a little."

"You shouldn't scare her. She's old."

"Dirt's old. Amie's a spring chicken." He chuckled. "Anyway, she was shopping for antique furniture on the Internet and she found a side table she couldn't live without in San Antonio. She drove up to look at it. She said she'd see me in a couple of days."

"And you're starving."

"You make the nicest scrambled eggs, Libby," he coaxed. "Nice crisp bacon. Delicious cinnamon toast. Strong coffee."

"It isn't the time of day for breakfast."

"No law that you can't have breakfast for supper," he pointed out.

She sighed. "I was planning a beef casserole."

"It won't go with scrambled eggs."

She put her hands on her hips and gave him a considering look. "You really are a pain, Jordan."

He moved a step closer and caught her by the waist with two big lean hands. "If you want me to marry you, you have to prove that you're a good cook."

"Marry…?"

Before she could get another word out, his mouth crushed down over her parted lips. He kissed her slowly, tenderly, his big hands steely at her waist, as if he were keeping them there by sheer will when he wanted to pull her body much closer to his own.

Her hands rested on his clean shirt while she tried to decide if he was kidding. He had to be. Certainly he didn't want to marry anybody. He'd said so often enough.

He lifted his head scant inches. "Stop doing that."

She blinked. "Doing what?"

"Thinking. You can't kiss a man and do analytical formulae in your head at the same time."

"You said you'd never marry anybody…."

His eyes were oddly solemn. "Maybe I changed my mind."

Before she could answer him, he bent his head and kissed her again. This time it wasn't a soft, teasing sample of a kiss. It was bold, brash, invasive and possessive. He enveloped her in his hard arms and crushed her down the length of his powerful body. She felt a husky groan go into her mouth as he grew more insistent.

Against her hips, she felt the sudden hardness of his body. As if he realized that and didn't like having her feel it, he moved away a breath. Slowly, he lifted his hard mouth from her swollen lips and looked down at her quietly, curiously.

"This is getting to be a habit," she said breathlessly. Her body was throbbing, like her heart. She wondered if he could hear it.

His dark eyes fell to the soft, quick pulsing of her heart, visible where her loose blouse bounced in time with it.

Beneath it, two hard little peaks were blatant. He saw them and his eyes began to glitter.

"Don't look at me like that," she whispered gruffly.

His eyes shot up to catch hers. "You want me," he said curtly. "I can see it. Feel it."

Her breath was audible. "You conceited…!"

His hands caught her hips and pushed them against his own. "It's mutual."

"I noticed!" she burst out, jerking away from him, red-faced.

"Don't be such a child," he chided, but gently. "You're old enough to know what desire feels like."

Her face grew redder. "I will not be seduced by you in my own kitchen over scrambled eggs!"

His eyebrows arched. "You're making them, then?" he asked brightly.

"Oh!" She pushed away from him. "You just won't take no for an answer!"

He smiled speculatively. "You can put butter on that," he agreed. His eyes went up and down her slender figure while she walked through to the kitchen, leaving her purse on the hall table as she went. "Not going to change before you start cooking?" he drawled, following her in. "I don't mind helping."

She shot him a dark glare.

He held up both hands. "Just offering to be helpful, that's all."

She laughed helplessly. "I can dress myself, thanks."

"I was offering to help you *un*dress," he pointed out.

She had to fight down another blush. She was a modern, independent woman. It was just that the thought of Jordan's dark eyes on her naked body had an odd, pleasurable effect on her. Especially after that bone-shaking kiss.

"You shouldn't go around kissing women like that unless you mean business," she pointed out as she got out a big iron skillet to cook the bacon in.

"What makes you think I didn't mean it?" he probed, straddling a kitchen chair to watch her work.

"You? Mr. I'll-Never-Marry?"

"I didn't say that. I said I didn't want to get married."

"Well, what's the difference?" she asked, exasperated.

His dark eyes slid down to her breasts with a boldness that made her uncomfortable. "There's always the one woman you can't walk away from."

"There's no such woman in your life."

"Think so?" He frowned. "What are you doing with that?" he asked as she put the skillet on the burner.

"You're the one who wanted bacon!" she exclaimed.

"Bacon, yes, not liquid fat!" He got up from the chair, pulled a couple of paper towels from the roll and pulled a plate from the cabinet. "Don't you know how to cook bacon?"

He proceeded to show her, layering several strips of bacon on a paper-towel coated plate and putting another paper towel on top of it.

She was watching with growing amusement. "And it's going to cook like that," she agreed. "Uh-huh."

"It goes in the microwave," he said with exaggerated patience. "You cook it for…"

"What's wrong?"

He was looking around, frowning, with the plate in one big hand. He opened cupboards and checked in the china cabinet. "All right, I'll bite. Where is it?"

"Where is what?"

"Your microwave oven!"

She sighed. "Jordan, we don't have a microwave oven."

"You're kidding." He scowled at her. "Everybody's got a microwave oven!"

"We haven't got one."

He studied her kitchen and slowly he put the plate back on the counter with a frown. The stove was at least ten years old. It was one of the old-fashioned ones that still had knobs instead of buttons. She didn't even have a dishwasher. Everything in the kitchen was old, like the cast-iron skillet she used for most every meal.

"I didn't realize how hard things were for you and Curt," he said after a minute. "I thought your father had all kinds of money."

"He did, until he married Janet," she replied. "She wanted to eat out all the time. The stove was worn out and so was the dishwasher. He was going to replace them, but she had him buy her a diamond ring she wanted, instead."

He scowled angrily. "I'm sorry. I'm really sorry."

His apology was unexpected and very touching. "It's all right," she said gently. "I'm used to doing things the hard way. Really I am."

He moved close, framing her oval face in his big warm hands. "You never complain."

She smiled. "Why should I? I'm healthy and strong and able to do anything that needs doing around here."

"You make me ashamed, Libby," he said softly. He bent and kissed her with aching tenderness.

"Why?" she whispered at his firm mouth.

"I'm not really sure. Do that again."

He nibbled her upper lip, coaxing her body to lean heavily against his. "This is even better than dessert," he murmured as he deepened the pressure of his mouth. "Come here!"

He lifted her against him and kissed her hungrily, until her mouth felt faintly bruised from the slow, insistent pressure. It was like flying. She loved kissing Jordan. She hoped he was never going to stop!

But all at once, he did, with a jerky breath. "This won't do," he murmured a little huskily. "Curt will be home any minute. I don't want him to find us on the kitchen table."

Her mouth flew open. "Jordan!"

He shrugged and looked sheepish. "It was heading that way. Here." He handed her the plate of bacon. "I guess you'd better fry it. I don't think it's going to cook by itself."

She smiled up at him. "I'll drain it on paper towels and get rid of some of the grease after it's cooked."

"Why are you throwing those away?" he asked when she put the bacon on to fry and threw away the paper towels it had laid on.

"Bacteria," she told him. "You never put meat back on a plate where it's been lying, raw."

"They teach you that in school these days, I guess?"

She nodded. "And lots of other stuff."

"Like how to use a prophylactic…?" he probed wickedly.

She flushed. "They did not! And I'll wash your mouth out with soap if you say that again!" she threatened.

"Never mind. I'll teach you how to use it, when the time comes," he added outrageously.

"I am not using a prophylactic!"

"You want kids right away, then?" he persisted.

"I am not having sex with you on my kitchen table!"

There was a sudden stunned silence. Jordan was staring over her shoulder and his expression was priceless. Grimacing, she turned to find her older brother standing there with his mouth open.

"Oh, shut your mouth, Curt," she grumbled. "It was a hypothetical discussion!"

"Except for the part about the prophylactic," Jordan said with a howling mad grin. "Did you know that they don't teach people how to use them in school?"

Curt lost it. He almost doubled over laughing.

Libby threw a dish towel at him. "Both of you, out of my kitchen! I'll call you when it's ready. Go on, out!"

They left the room obediently, still laughing.

Libby shook her head and started turning the bacon.

"Hasn't Janet even phoned to say if she was coming back today?" Jordan asked the two siblings when they were seated at the kitchen table having supper.

"There wasn't anything on the answering machine,"

Libby said. "I checked it while the bacon was cooking. Maybe she thinks we're on to something and she's running for it."

"No, I don't think so," Curt replied at once. "She's not about to leave this property to us. Not considering what it would be worth to a developer."

"I agree," Jordan said. "I've given Kemp the phone number of a private detective I know in San Antonio," he added. "He's going to look into the case for me."

"We'll pay you back," Curt promised, and Libby nodded.

"Let's cross our bridges one at a time," Jordan replied. "First order of business is to see if we can find any proof that she's committed a crime in the past."

"Mabel said she was suspected in a death at a nursing home in Branntville," she volunteered.

"So Kemp told me," Jordan said. "This is good bacon," he added.

"Thanks," she said with a smile.

"Violet's father was another one of her victims," Libby added.

Jordan nodded while Curt scowled curiously at both of them. "But they can't prove that. Not unless there's enough evidence to order an exhumation. And, considering the physical condition of Violet's mother," he added, "I'm afraid she'd never be able to agree to it. The shock would probably kill her mother."

Libby sighed. "Poor Violet. She's had such a hard life. And now to have to change jobs…"

"She works for Kemp, doesn't she?" Curt asked.

"She did. She quit today," Libby replied. "She's going to work for Duke Wright."

"Oh, Sherry King's going to *love* that," Curt chuckled.

"She doesn't own Duke," Libby said. "He doesn't even like her."

"She's very possessive about men she wants."

"More power to her if she can put a net over him and lock him in her closet."

Jordan chuckled. "He's not keen on the thought of a second wife."

"He's still trying to get custody of his son, isn't he?" Curt asked. "Poor guy."

"He won't be the first man who lost a woman to a career," Jordan reminded him. "Although it's usually the other way around." He glanced at Libby. "Just for the record, I think you're more important than a new bull, no matter what his ancestry is."

"Gee, thanks," she replied, tongue-in-cheek.

"It never hurts to clear up these little details before they become issues," he said wryly. "On the other hand, it would be nice if you'd tell me if you have plans to go to law school and move to a big city to practice law?"

"Not me, thanks," she replied. "I'm very happy where I am."

"You don't know any other life except this one," he persisted. "What if you regret not spreading your wings further on down the road?"

"We can't see into the future, Jordan," she replied thoughtfully. "But I don't like cities, although I'm sure they're exciting for some people. I don't like parties or business and I wouldn't trade jobs with Kemp for anything on earth. I'm happy looking up case precedents and researching options. I wouldn't like having to stand up in a courtroom and argue a case."

"You don't know that," he mused, and a shadow crossed his face. "What if you got a taste of it one day and couldn't live without it but it was too late?"

"Too late?"

"What if you had kids and a husband?" he prompted.

"You're thinking about Duke Wright," she said slowly.

He drew in a hard breath, aware that Curt was watching him curiously. "Yes," he told her. "Duke's wife was a secretary. She took night courses to get her law degree and then got pregnant just before she started practice. While Duke was giving bottles and changing diapers, she was climbing the ladder at a prestigious San Antonio law firm, living there during the week and coming home on weekends. Then they offered her a job in New York City.''

Libby couldn't quite figure out the look on his face. He was taking it all quite seriously and she'd thought he was teasing.

"So you see," he continued, "she didn't know she wanted a career until it was too late. Now she's making a six-figure annual income and their little boy's in her way. She doesn't want to give him up, but she doesn't have time to take care of him properly. And Duke's caught in the middle.''

"I hadn't realized it was that bad," she confessed. "Poor Duke.''

"He had a choice," he told her. "He married her thinking she wanted what he did, a nice home and a comfortable living, and kids.'' He drew a breath. "But she was very young," he added, his eyes studying her covertly. "Maybe she didn't really know what she wanted. Then.''

"I suppose some women don't," she replied. "It's a new world. Maybe it took her a long time to realize the opportunities and then it was too late to go back.''

He lowered his eyes to his boots. "That's very possible.''

"But it's Duke's problem," she added, smiling. "Want some pie? I've got a cherry one that I made yesterday in the refrigerator.''

He shook his head. "Thanks. But I won't stay." He got to his feet. "I'll tell Kemp to let you know what the private detective finds out. Meanwhile," he added, glancing at Curt, "not a word to Janet. Okay?''

They both nodded.

"Thanks, Jordan," Curt added.

"What are neighbors for?" he replied, and he chuckled. But his eyes didn't quite meet Libby's.

* * *

"Jordan was acting very oddly tonight, wasn't he?" Libby asked her brother after they'd washed the dishes and put them away.

"He's a man with a lot on his mind," he replied. "Calhoun Ballenger's making a very powerful bid for that senate seat that old man Merrill's had for so many years. They say old man Merrill's worried and so's his daughter, Julie. You remember, she's been pursuing Jordan lately."

"But he and Calhoun have been friendly for years," she said.

"So they have. There's more. Old man Merrill got pulled over for drunk driving by a couple of our local cops. Now Merrill's pulling strings at city hall to try and make the officers withdraw the charges. Merrill doesn't have a lot of capital. Jordan does."

"Surely you don't think Jordan would go against Cash Grier, even for Julie?" she wondered, concerned.

He started to speak and then thought better of it. "I'm not sure I really know," he said.

She rubbed at a clean plate thoughtfully. "Do you suppose he's serious about her? She and her father are very big socially and they have a house here that they stay in from time to time. She has a college degree. In fact, they say she may try her hand at politics. He was talking about marriage and children to us—like he was serious about it." She frowned. "Does that kind of woman settle down? Or was that what he meant, when he said some women don't know what they want until they find it?"

"I don't know that he's got marriage on his mind," Curt replied slowly. "But he's spent a good deal of time with Julie and the senator just lately."

That hurt. She bit her lower lip, hard, and forced her mind away from the heat and power of Jordan's kisses. "We've got a problem of our own. What are we going to do about Janet?"

"Kemp's working on that, isn't he? And Jordan's private detective will be working with him. They'll turn up some-

thing. She isn't going to put us out on the street, Libby,"
he said gently. "I promise you she isn't."

She smiled up at him. "You're sort of nice, for a
brother."

He grinned. "Glad you noticed!"

She didn't sleep all night, though, wondering about Jordan's odd remarks and the way he'd looked at her when
he asked if she had ambitions toward law practice. She
really didn't, but he seemed to think she was too young to
know her own mind.

Well, it wasn't really anything to worry about, she assured herself. Jordan had no idea of marrying *her,* regardless of her ambition or lack thereof. But Curt had said he
was seeing a lot of Julie Merrill. For some unfathomable
reason, the thought made her sad.

Chapter Four

It was late afternoon before Janet came back, looking out of sorts. She threw herself onto the sofa in the living room and lit a cigarette.

"You'll stink up the place," Libby muttered, hunting for an ashtray. She put it on the table.

"Well, then, you'll have to invest in some more air freshener, won't you, darling?" the older woman asked coldly.

Libby stared at her angrily. "Where have you been for three days?"

Janet avoided looking at her. "I had some business to settle."

"It had better not have been any sales concerning this property," Libby told her firmly.

"And who's going to stop me?" the other woman demanded hotly.

"Mr. Kemp."

Janet crushed out the cigarette and got to her feet. "Let him try. You try, too! I own everything here and I'm not letting you take it away from me! No matter what I have

to do," she added darkly. "I earned what I'm getting, putting up with your father handling me like a live doll. The
repulsive old fool made my skin crawl!"

"My father loved you," Libby bit off, furious that the
awful woman could make such a remark about her father,
the kindest man she'd ever known.

"He loved showing me off, you mean," Janet muttered.
"If he'd really loved me, he'd have given me the things I
asked him for. But he was so cheap! Well, I'm not being
cheated out of what's mine," she added, with a cold glare
at Libby. "Not by you or your brother. I have a lawyer,
too, now."

Libby felt sick. But she managed a calm smile. "We
have locks on our bedroom doors, by the way," she said
out of the blue. "And Mr. Kemp is having a private detective check you out."

Janet looked shocked. "W-what?"

"Violet who works in my office thinks you might have
known her father— Mr. Hardy from San Antonio?" she
added deliberately. "He had a heart attack, just like
Daddy…?"

Janet actually went pale. She jumped to her feet as if
she'd been stung.

"Where are you going?" Libby asked seconds later,
when the older woman rushed from the room.

Janet went into her bedroom and slammed the door. The
sound of objects bouncing off walls followed in a furious
staccato.

Libby bit her lip. She'd been warned not to do anything
to make Janet panic and make a run for it, but the woman
had pricked her temper. She wished she hadn't opened her
mouth.

With dark thoughts, she finished baking a ham and made
potato salad to go with it, along with homemade rolls. It
gave her something to do besides worry.

But when Curt came home to eat, he was met by Janet
with a suitcase, going out the door.

"Where are you off to?" he asked her coolly.

She threw a furious glance at the kitchen. "Anywhere I don't have to put up with your sister!" she snarled. "I'll get a motel room in town. You'll be hearing from my attorney in a day or so."

Curt's eyebrows lifted. "Funny. I was just about to tell you the same thing. I had a phone call from Kemp while I was at work. His private investigator has turned up some *very* interesting information about your former employment at a nursing home in Branntville…?"

Janet brushed by him in a mad rush toward her Mercedes. She threw her case in and jumped in behind it, spraying dirt as she spun out of the driveway.

"Well, that's clinched it," Curt mused as he joined his troubled sister in the kitchen. "She won't be back, or I'll miss my bet."

"I don't think it was a good idea to run her off," she commented as she set the table. "I'd already opened my big mouth and mentioned the locks on our bedroom doors and Violet's father to her."

"It's okay," Curt said gently. "I'm doing what Kemp told me to. I put her on the run."

"Mr. Kemp said to do that?"

He nodded, tossing his hat onto a side table and pulling out a chair. "Any coffee going? We've been mucking out line cabins all day. I'm beat!"

"Mucking out line cabins, not stables?"

"The river ran out of its banks right into that cabin on the north border," he said heavily. "We've been shoveling mud all afternoon. Crazy, isn't it? We had drought for four years, now it's floods. God must really be mad at somebody!"

"Don't look at me, I haven't done a single thing out of line."

He smiled. "When have you ever?" He studied her as she put food on the table. "Jordan says he's taking you out to a movie next week…watch it!"

Her hands almost let go of the potato salad bowl. She caught it and put it down carefully, gaping at her brother. "Jordan's taking *me* to a movie?"

"It's what usually happens when men start kissing women," he said philosophically, leaning back in his chair with a wicked grin. "They get addicted."

"How did you know he was kissing me last night?"

He grinned wickedly. "I didn't."

She cleared her throat and turned away, reddening as she remembered the passionate kiss she and Jordan had shared before the supper he'd coaxed her to cook for him. She hadn't slept well all night thinking about it. Or about what Curt had said, that Jordan was spending a lot of time with Julie Merrill. But he couldn't be interested in the woman, if he wanted to take Libby out!

"You never got addicted to any women," she pointed out.

He shrugged. "My day will come. It just hasn't yet."

"What were you telling Janet about a private investigator and the nursing home?"

"Oh, yes." He waited until she sat down and they said grace before he continued, while piling ham on his plate. "I'm not sure how much Kemp told you already but it seems that Janet has changed her legal identity since she worked in the nursing home. Also her hair color. She was under suspicion for the death of that elderly patient who liked to play the horses. She was making off with his bank account when it seems she was paid a visit by a gentleman representing a rather shadowy figure who was owed a great deal of money by the deceased. She left everything and ran for her life." He smiled complacently. "You see, there were more debts than money left in the elderly gentleman's entire estate!"

Libby was listening intently.

"There's more." He took a bite of ham. "This is nice!" he exclaimed when he tasted it.

"Isn't it?" She smiled. "I got it from Duke Wright. He's

sidelining into a pork products shop and he's marketing on the Internet. He's doing organic bacon and ham.''

"Smart guy."

She nodded. "There's more, you said?''

"Yes. They've just managed to convince Violet's mother that her husband might have been murdered. She's agreed to an exhumation.''

"But they said the shock might be fatal!''

"Mrs. Hardy loved her husband. She never believed it was a heart attack. He'd had an echocardiogram that was misread, leading to a heart catheterization. They found nothing that would indicate grounds for a heart attack.''

"Poor Violet," Libby said sadly. "It's going to be hard on her, too.'' She glanced up at her brother. "I still can't believe she quit and is going to work for Duke Wright.''

"I know," he said. "She was crazy about Kemp!''

She nodded sadly. "Serves him right. He's been unpleasant to her lately. Violet's tired of eating her heart out for him. And who knows. It might prompt Mr. Kemp to do some soul searching.''

"More than likely he'll just hire somebody else and forget all about her. If he wanted to be married, he could be,'' he added.

"He doesn't date anybody, does he?'' she asked curiously.

He shook his head. "But he's not gay.''

"I never thought he was. I just wondered why he keeps so much to himself.''

"Maybe he's like a lot of other bachelors in Jacobsville, he's got a secret past that he doesn't want to share!''

"We're running out of bachelors," she retorted. "The Hart boys were the last to go and nobody ever thought they'd end up with families.''

"Biscuits were their downfall," he pointed out.

"Jordan doesn't like biscuits," she mused. "I did ask, you know.''

He chuckled. "Jordan doesn't have a weakness and he's

never lacked dates when he wanted them." He eyed her over his coffee cup. "But he may be at the end of his own rope."

"Don't look at me," she said, having spent too much time lately thinking about Jordan's intentions toward her. "I may be the flavor of the week, but Jordan isn't going to want to marry down, if you see what I mean."

His eyes narrowed. "We may not be high society, but our people go back a long way in Jacobs County."

"That doesn't put us in monied circles, either," she reminded him. Her eyes were dreamy and faraway. "He's got a big, fancy house and he likes to keep company with high society. Maybe that's why he's been taking Senator Merrill's daughter around. It gets him into places he was never invited to before. We'd never fit. Especially me," she added in a more wistful tone than she realized.

"That wouldn't matter."

She smiled sadly. "It would and you know it. He'll need a wife who can entertain and throw parties, arrange sales, things like that. Most of all, he'll want a woman who's beautiful and intelligent, someone he'll be proud to show off. He might take me to a movie. But believe me, he won't take me to a minister."

"You're sure of that?"

She looked up at him. "You said it yourself— Jordan has been spending a lot of time with the state senator's daughter. He's running for re-election and the latest polls say that Calhoun Ballenger is almost tied with him. He needs all the support he can get, financial and otherwise. I think Jordan's going to help him, because of Julie."

"Then why is he kissing you?"

"To make her jealous?" she pondered. "Maybe to convince himself that he's still attractive to women. But it's not serious. Not with him." She looked up. "And I don't have affairs, whether it's politically correct or not."

He sighed. "I suppose we all have our pipe dreams."

"What's yours, while we're on the subject?"

He smiled. "I'd like to start a ranch supply company. The last one left belonged to Ted Regan's father-in-law. When he died, the store went bust, and then his daughter Corrie married Ted Regan and didn't need to make her own living. The hardware store can order most supplies, but not cattle feed or horse feed. Stuff like that."

She hadn't realized her brother had such ambitions. "If we weren't in such a financial mess, I'd be more than willing to co-sign a loan with the house as collateral."

He stared at her intently. "You'd do that for me?"

"Of course. You're my brother. I love you."

He reached out and caught her hand. "I love you, too, Sis."

"Pipe dreams are nice. Don't you give yours up. Eventually we'll settle this inheritance question and we might have a little capital to work with." She studied him with pride. "I think you'd make a great success of it. You've kept us solvent, up until Janet's unexpected arrival."

"She'll be out for blood. I should probably call Kemp and update him on what's happened."

"That might not be a bad idea. Maybe we should get a dog," she added slowly.

"Bad idea. We can hardly afford to feed old Bailey, your horse. We'd have to buy food for a dog, too, and it would break us."

She saw his eyes twinkle and she burst out laughing, too.

Janet's attorney never showed up and two days later, Janet vanished, leaving a trail of charges to the Collinses for everything from clothes to the motel bill.

"You won't have to pay that," Kemp told Libby when he'd related the latest news to her. "I've already alerted the merchants that she had no authority to charge anything to you or Curt, or the estate."

"Thanks," she said with relief. "What do we do now?"

"I've got the state police out looking for her," he replied, his hands deep in his slacks' pockets. "On suspicion of murder. You won't like what's coming next."

"What?"

"I want to have your father exhumed."

She ground her teeth together. "I was afraid of that."

"We'll be discreet. But we need to have the crime lab check for trace evidence of poisoning. You see, we know what killed the old man at the nursing home where she worked. I believe she did kill him. Poisoners tend to stick to the same routine."

"Poor Daddy," she said, feeling sick. Now she wondered if they might have saved him, if they'd only realized sooner that Janet was dangerous.

"Don't play mind games with yourself, Libby," Kemp said quietly. "It does no good."

"What a terrible way to go."

"The poison she used was quick," he replied. "Some can cause symptoms for months and the victim dies a painfully slow death. That wasn't the case here. It's the only good news I have for you, I'm afraid. But after they autopsy Mr. Hardy, there may be more forensic evidence to make a case against her. We've found a source for the poison."

"But the doctor said that Daddy died of a heart attack," she began.

"He might have," Kemp had to admit. "But he could as easily have died of poison or an air embolism."

"Jordan mentioned that," she recalled.

He smiled secretively. "Jordan doesn't miss a trick."

"But Janet's gone. What if they discover that Daddy's death was foul play and then they can't find her?" Libby pointed out. "She's gotten away with it at least two times, by being cagey."

"Every criminal eventually makes a mistake," he said absently. "She'll make one. Mark my words."

She only nodded. She glanced at Violet's empty desk and winced.

"I have an ad in the paper for a new secretary," he said coldly. "Meanwhile, Mabel's going to do double duty," he added, nodding toward Mabel, who was on the phone taking notes.

"It's going to be lonely without her," she said without thinking.

Kemp actually ground his teeth, turned on his heel and went back into his office. As an afterthought, he slammed the door.

Libby lost it. She laughed helplessly. Mabel, off the phone now and aware of Kemp's shocking attitude, laughed, too.

"It won't last long," Mabel whispered. "Violet was the only secretary he's ever had who could make and break appointments without hurting people's feelings. She was the fastest typist, too. He's not going to find somebody to replace her overnight."

Libby agreed silently. But it promised to be an interesting working environment for the foreseeable future.

Libby didn't even notice there was a message on the answering machine until after supper, when she'd had a lonely sandwich after Curt had phoned and said he was eating pizza with the other cowboys over at the Regan place for their weekly card game.

Curious, Libby punched the answer key and listened to the message. In a silken tone, the caller identified himself as an attorney named Smith and said that Mrs. Collins had hired him to do the probate on her late husband's will. He added that the children of Riddle Collins would have two weeks to vacate the premises.

Libby went through the roof. Her hands trembled as she tried to call Kemp and failing to reach him, she punched in Jordan's number.

It took a long time for him to answer the phone and when he finally did, there was conversation and music in the background.

"Yes?" he asked curtly.

Libby faltered. "Am I interrupting? I can call you another time…"

"Libby?" His voice softened. "Wait a minute." She heard muffled conversation, an angry reply, and the sound of a door closing. "Okay," he said. "What's wrong?"

"I can't get Mr. Kemp," she began urgently, "and Janet's attorney just called and said we had two weeks to get out of the house before they did the probate!"

"Libby," he said softly, "just sit down and use your mind. Think. When has anybody ever been asked to vacate a house just so that probate papers could be filed?"

She took a deep breath and then another. Her hands were still cold and trembling but she was beginning to remember bits and pieces of court documents. She was a paralegal. For God's sake, she knew about probate!

She sighed heavily. "Thanks. I just lost it. I was so shocked and so scared!"

"Is Curt there?"

"No, he went to his weekly card game with the cowboys over at Ted Regan's ranch," she said.

"I'm sorry I can't come over and talk to you. I'm having a fund-raising party for Senator Merrill tonight."

Merrill. His daughter Julie was the socialite. She was beautiful and rich and…socially acceptable. Certainly, she'd be at the party, too.

"Libby?" he prompted, when she didn't answer him.

"That's…that's okay, Jordan, I don't need company, honest," she said at once. "I just lost my mind for a minute. I'm sorry I bothered you. Really!"

"You don't have to apologize," he said, as if her statement unsettled him.

"I'll hang up now. Thanks, Jordan!"

He was still talking when she put the receiver down, very quickly, and put the answering machine back on. If he called back, she wasn't answering him. Janet's vicious tactics had unsettled her. She knew Janet had gotten someone to make that phone call deliberately, to upset Riddle's children.

It was her way of getting even, no doubt, for what Libby and Curt had said to her. She wondered if there was any way they could trace a call off an answering machine? A flash of inspiration hit her. Before Jordan would have time to call and foul the connection, she jerked up the phone and pressed the *69 keys. It gave her the number of the party who'd just phoned and she wrote it down at once, delighted to see that it was not a local number. She'd give it to Kemp the next morning and let his private investigator look into it.

Feeling more confident, she went back to the kitchen and finished washing up the few dishes. She couldn't forget Jordan's deep voice on the phone and the sound of a woman's voice arguing angrily when he went into another room to talk to Libby. It must be that senator's daughter. Obviously she felt possessive of Jordan and was wary of any potential rival. But Libby was no rival, she told herself. Jordan had just kissed her. That was all.

If only she could forget how it had felt. Then she re-membered something else: Jordan's odd statements about Duke Wright's wife, and how young she was, and how she didn't quite know she wanted a career until she was already married and pregnant. He'd given Libby an odd, searching look when he said that.

The senator's daughter, Julie Merrill, was twenty-six, she recalled, with a degree in political science. Obviously she already knew what she wanted. She wanted Jordan. She was at his house tonight, probably hostessing the party there. Libby looked down at her worn jeans and faded blouse and then around her at the shabby but useful fur-niture in the old house. She laughed mirthlessly. What in the world would Jordan want with her, anyway? She'd been daydreaming. She'd better wake up, before she had her heart torn out.

* * *

She didn't phone Jordan again and he didn't call her back. She did give the telephone number of the so-called attorney to Mr. Kemp, who passed it along to his investigator.

Several days later, he paused by Libby's desk while she was writing up a precedent for a libel case, and he looked smug.

"That was quick thinking on your part," he remarked with a smile. "We traced the number to San Antonio. The man isn't an attorney, though. He's a waiter in a high-class restaurant who thinks Janet is his meal ticket to the easy life. We, uh, disabused him of the idea and told him one of her possible futures. We understand that he quit his job and left town on the next bus to make sure he wasn't involved in anything she did."

She laughed softly. "Thank goodness! Then Curt and I don't have to move!"

Kemp glared at her. "As if I'd stand by and let any so-called attorney toss you out of your home!"

"Thanks, boss," she said with genuine gratitude.

He shrugged. "Paralegals are thin on the ground," he said with twinkling blue-gray eyes.

"Callie Kirby and I are the only ones that I know of in town right now," she agreed.

"And Callie's got a child," he said, nodding. "I don't think Micah's going to want her to come back to work until their kids are in school."

"I expect not. She's got Micah's father to help take care of, too," she added, "after his latest stroke."

"People die," he said, and his eyes seemed distant and troubled.

"Mabel called in sick," she said reluctantly. "She's got some sort of stomach virus."

"They go around every spring," he agreed with a sigh. "Can you handle everything, or do you want to get a temp? If you do, call the agency. Ask if they've got somebody who can type."

She gave him her most innocent look. "Of course I can do the work of three women, sir, and even make coffee…"

He laughed. "Call the agency."

"Yes, sir."

He glowered. "It's Violet's fault," he muttered, turning. "I'll bet she's cursed us. We'll have sick help from now on."

"I'm sure she'd never do that, Mr. Kemp," she assured him. "She's a nice person."

"Imagine taking offense at a *look* and throwing in the towel. Hell, I look at people all the time and they don't quit!"

She cleared her throat and nodded toward the door, which was just opening.

A lovely young woman with a briefcase and long blond hair came in. "I'm Julie Merrill," she said with a haughty smile. "Senator Merrill's daughter? You advertised for a secretary, I believe."

Libby could not believe her eyes. Jordan's latest love and she turned up here looking for work! Of all the horrible bad luck…

Kemp stared at the young woman without speaking.

"Oh, not me!" Julie laughed, clearing her throat. "Heavens, I don't need a job! No, it's my friend Lydia. She's just out of secretarial school and she can't find anything suitable."

"Can she type?"

"Yes! Sixty words a minute. And she can take shorthand, if you don't dictate too fast."

"Can she speak?"

Julie blinked. "I beg your pardon?"

Kemp gave her a scrutiny that would have stopped traffic. His eyes became a wintry blue, which Libby knew from experience meant that his temper was just beginning to kindle.

"I don't give jobs through third persons, Miss Merrill,

and I don't give a damn who your father is," he said with a cool smile.

She colored hotly and gaped at him. "I...I...just thought...I mean, I could ask...!"

"Tell your friend she can come in and fill out an application, but not to expect much," he added shortly. "I have no respect for a woman who has to be helped into a job through favoritism. And in case it's escaped your attention," he added, moving a step closer to her, "nobody works for me unless they're qualified."

Julie shot a cold glare at Libby, who was watching intently. "I guess you think she's qualified," she said angrily.

"I have a diploma as a trained paralegal," Libby replied coolly. "It's on the wall behind you, at my desk."

Kemp only smiled. It wasn't a nice smile.

Julie set her teeth together so hard that they almost clicked. "I don't think Lydia would like this job, anyway!"

Kemp's right eyebrow arched. "Was there anything else, Miss Merrill?"

She turned, jerking open the door. "My father will not be happy when I tell him how you've spoken to me."

"By all means, tell him, with my blessing," Kemp said. "One of his faults is a shameful lack of discipline with his children. I understand you've recently expressed interest in running for public office in Jacobs County, Miss Merrill. Let me give you a piece of advice. Don't."

Her mouth fell open. "How dare you...!"

"It's your father's money, of course. If he wants to throw it away, that's his concern."

"I could win an election!"

Kemp smiled. "Perhaps you could. But not in Jacobs County," he said pleasantly. His eyes narrowed and became cold and his voice grew deceptively soft. "Closet skeletons become visible baggage in an election. And no one here has forgotten your high-school party. Especially not the Culbertsons."

Julie's face went pale. Her fingers on the briefcase

tightened until the knuckles showed. She actually looked frightened.

"That was…a terrible accident."

"Shannon Culbertson is still dead."

Julie's lower lip trembled. She turned and went out the door so quickly that she forgot to close it.

Kemp did it for her, his face cold and hard, full of repressed fury.

Libby wondered what was going on, but she didn't dare ask.

Later, of course, when Curt got home from work, she couldn't resist asking the question.

He scowled. "What the hell did Julie want in Kemp's office? Lydia doesn't need a job, she already has a job—a good one—at the courthouse over in Bexar County!"

"She said Lydia wanted to work for Mr. Kemp, but she was giving me the evil eye for all she was worth."

"She wants Jordan. You're in the way."

"Sure I am," she laughed coldly. "What about that girl, Shannon Culbertson?"

Curt hesitated. "That was eight years ago."

"What happened?"

"Somebody put something in her drink—which she wasn't supposed to have had in the first place. It was a forerunner of the date-rape drug. She had a hidden heart condition. It killed her."

"Who did it?"

"Nobody knows, but Julie tried to cover it up, to save her father's senate seat. Kemp dug out the truth and gave it to the newspapers." He shook his head. "A vindictive man, Kemp."

"Why?" she asked.

"They say Kemp was in love with the girl. He never got over it."

"But Julie's father won the election," she pointed out.

"Only because the leading lights of the town supported him and contributed to his reelection campaign. Most of those old-timers are dead or in nursing homes and the gossip around town is that Senator Merrill is already over his ears in debt from his campaign. Besides which, he's up against formidable opposition for the first time in recent years.''

Chapter Five

So that was Kemp's secret, Libby thought. A lost love. "Yes, I know," she said. "Calhoun Ballenger has really shaken up the district politically. A lot of people think he's going to win the nomination right out from under Merrill."

"I'm almost sure he will," Curt replied. "The powers that be in the county have changed over the past few years. The Harts have come up in the world. So have the Tremaynes, the Ballengers, Ted Regan, and a few other families. The power structure now isn't in the hands of the old elite. If you don't believe that, notice what's going on at city hall. Chief Grier is making a record number of drug busts and I don't need to remind you that Senator Merrill was arrested for drunk driving."

"That never was in the paper, you know," she said with a wry smile.

"The publisher is one of his cronies—he refused to run the story. But Merrill's up to his ears in legal trouble. So he's trying to get the mayor and two councilmen who owe him favors to fire the two police officers who made the arrest and discredit them. The primary election is the first week of May, you know.''

''Poor police,'' she murmured.

''Mark my words, they'll never lose their jobs. Grier has contacts everywhere and despite his personal problems, he's not going to let his officers go down without a fight. I'd bet everything I have on him.''

She grinned. ''I like him.''

Curt chuckled. ''I like him, too.''

''Mr. Kemp said they traced the lawyer's call to San Antonio,'' she added, and told him what was said. ''Why would she want us out of the house?''

''Maybe she thinks there's something in it that she hasn't gotten yet,'' he mused. ''Dad's coin collection, for instance.''

''I haven't seen that in months,'' she said.

''Neither have I. She probably sold it already,'' he said with cold disgust. ''But Janet's going to hang herself before she quits.'' He gave his sister a sad look. ''I'm sorry about the exhumation. But we really need to know the truth about how Dad died.''

''I know,'' she replied. The pain was still fresh and she had to fight tears. She managed a smile for him. ''Daddy wouldn't mind.''

''No. I don't think he would.''

''I wish we'd paid more attention to what was going on.''

''He thought he loved her, Libby,'' he said. ''Maybe he did. He wouldn't have listened to us, no matter what we said, if it was something bad about her. You know how he was.''

''Loving her blindly may have cost him his life.''

''Try to remember that he died happy. He didn't know what Janet was. He didn't know that she was cheating him.''

''It doesn't help much.''

He nodded. ''Nothing will bring him back. But maybe

we can save somebody else's father. That would make it all worthwhile.''

"Yes," she agreed. "It would."

That evening while they were watching television, a truck drove up. A minute later, there was a hard knock on the door.

"I've got it," Curt said, leaving Libby with her embroidery.

There were muffled voices and then heavy footsteps coming into the room.

Jordan stared at Libby curiously. "Julie came to your office today," he said.

"She was looking for a job for her friend Lydia," Libby said in a matter-of-fact tone.

"That's not what she said," Jordan replied tersely. "She told me that you treated her so rudely that Kemp made her leave the office."

Libby lifted both eyebrows. "Wow. Imagine that."

"I'm not joking with you, Libby," Jordan said, and his tone chilled. "That was a petty thing to do."

"It would have been," she agreed, growing angry herself, "if I'd done it. She came into the office in a temper, glared at me, made some rude remarks to Mr. Kemp and got herself thrown out."

"That's not what she told me," he repeated.

Libby got to her feet, motioning to Curt, who was about to protest on her behalf. "I don't need help, Curt. Stay out of it, that's a nice brother." She moved closer to Jordan. "Miss Merrill insinuated that Mr. Kemp had better offer Lydia a job because of her father's position in the community. And he reminded her about her high-school graduation party where a girl died."

"He what?" he exploded.

"Mr. Kemp doesn't take threats lying down," she said, uneasy because of Jordan's overt hostility. "Miss Merrill was very haughty and very rude. And neither of us can understand why she'd try to get Lydia a job at Kemp's office, because she's already got one in San Antonio!''

Jordan didn't say anything. He just stood there, silent.

"She was with you when I phoned your house, I guess, and she got the idea that I was chasing you," she said, gratified by the sudden blinking of his eyelids. "You can tell her, for me," she added with saccharine sweetness, "that I would not have you on a hot dog bun with uptown relish. If she thinks I'm the competition, all she has to do is look where I live." Her face tautened. "Go ahead, Jordan, look around you. I'm not even in your league, whatever your high-class girlfriend thinks. You're a kind neighbor whom I asked for advice and that's all you ever were. Period," she lied, trying to save face.

He still wasn't moving or speaking. But his eyes were taking on a nasty glitter. Beside his lean hips, one of his hands was clenched until the knuckles went white. "Ever?" he prodded, his tone insinuating things.

She knew what he meant. She swallowed hard, trying not to remember the heat and power of the kisses they'd shared. Obviously, they'd meant nothing to him!

"Ever," she repeated. "I certainly wasn't trying to tie you down, Jordan. I'm not at all sure that I want to spend the rest of my life in Jacobsville working for a lawyer, anyway," she added deliberately, but without looking at him. "I've thought about that a lot, about what you said. Maybe I do have ambitions."

He didn't speak for several seconds. His eyes became narrow and cold.

"If you'd like to show your Julie that I'm no competition, you can bring her down here and show her how we live," she offered with a smile. "That would really open her eyes, wouldn't it?"

"Libby," Curt warned. "Don't talk like that."

"How should I talk?" she demanded, her throat tightening. "Our father is dead and it looks like our stepmother killed him right under our noses! She's trying to take away everything we have, getting her friends to call and threaten and harass us, and now here's Jordan's goody-two-shoes girlfriend making me out to be a man-stealer, or somebody. How the hell should I talk?!''

Jordan let out a long breath. ''I thought you knew what you wanted,'' he said after a minute.

''I'm young. Like you said,'' she said cynically. ''Sorry I ever asked you for help, Jordan, and made your girlfriend mad. You can bet I'll never make that mistake twice.''

She turned and went into the kitchen and slammed the door behind her. She was learning really bad habits from Mr. Kemp, she decided, as she wiped tears away with a paper towel.

She heard the door open behind her and close again, firmly. It was Curt, she supposed, coming to check on her.

''I guess I handled that badly,'' she said, choking on tears. ''Has he gone?''

Big, warm hands caught her shoulders and turned her around. Jordan's eyes glittered down into hers. ''No, he hasn't gone,'' he bit off.

He looked ferocious like that. She should have been intimidated, but she wasn't. He was handsome, even bristling with temper.

''I've said all I have to say,'' she began.

''Well, I haven't,'' he shot back, goaded. ''I've never looked down on you for what you've got and you know it.''

''Julie Merrill does,'' she muttered.

His hands tightened and relaxed. He looked vaguely embarrassed. His dark eyes slid past her to the worn calendar on the wall. ''You know how I grew up,'' he said heavily. ''We had nothing. I was never invited to parties. My parents were glorified servants in the eyes of the town's social set.''

She drew in a short breath. ''And now Julie's opening the doors and inviting you in and you like it.''

He seemed shocked by the statement. His eyes dropped to meet hers. "Maybe."

"Can't you see why?" she asked quietly. "You're rich now. You made something out of nothing. You have confidence, and power, and you know how to behave in company. But there's more to it than that, where the Merrills are concerned."

"That's not your business," he said shortly.

She smiled sadly. "They need financial backing. Their old friends aren't as wealthy as they used to be. Calhoun Ballenger has the support of the newer wealthy people in Jacobsville and they don't deal in 'good old boy' politics."

"In other words, Julie only wants me for money to run her father's re-election campaign."

"You know better than that," she replied, searching his hard face hungrily. "You're handsome and sexy. Women adore you."

One eyebrow lifted. "Even you?"

She wanted to deny it, but she couldn't. "Even me," she confessed. "But I'm no more in your class, really, than you're in Julie's. They're old money. It doesn't really matter to them how rich you get, you'll never be one of them."

His eyes narrowed angrily. "I am one of them," he retorted. "I'm hobnobbing with New York society, with Kentucky thoroughbred breeders, with presidential staff members—even with Hollywood producers and actors!"

"You could do that on your own," she said. "You don't need the Merrills to make you socially acceptable. And in case you've forgotten, Christabel and Judd Dunn have been hobnobbing with Hollywood people for a year. They're not rich. Not really."

He was losing the argument and he didn't like it. He glared down at her with more riotous feelings than he'd entertained in years. "Julie wants to marry me," he said, producing the flat statement like a weapon.

She managed not to react to the retort, barely. Her heart was sinking like lead in her chest as she pictured Julie in a designer wedding gown flashing diamonds like pennies on her way to the altar.

"*She* doesn't want a career," he added, smiling coldly.

Neither did Libby, really. She liked having a job, but she also liked living in Jacobsville and working around the ranch. She'd have liked being Jordan's wife more than anything else she could think of. But that wasn't going to happen. He didn't want her.

She tried to pull away from Jordan's strong hands, but he wasn't budging.

"Let me go," she muttered. "I'm sure Julie wouldn't like this!"

"Wouldn't like what?" he drawled. "Being in my arms, or having you in them?"

"Are you having fun?" she challenged.

"Not yet," he murmured, dropping his gaze to her full lips. "But I expect to be pretty soon…"

"You can't…!"

But he could. And he was. She felt the warm, soft, coaxing pressure of his hard mouth before she could finish the protest. Her eyes closed. She was aware of his size and strength, of the warmth of his powerful body against hers. She could feel his heartbeat, feel the rough sigh of his breath as he deepened the kiss.

He hadn't really meant to do this. He'd meant it as a punishment, for the things she'd said to him. But when he had her so close that he could feel her heart beating like a wild thing against him, nothing else seemed to matter except pleasing her, as she was pleasing him.

He drew her up closer, so that he could feel the soft, warm imprint of her body on the length of his. He traced her soft mouth with his lips, with the tip of his tongue. He felt her stiffen and then lift up to him. He gathered her completely against him and forgot Julie, forgot the argument, forgot everything.

She felt the sudden ardor of his embrace grow unmanageable in a space of seconds. His mouth was insistent on hers, demanding. His hands had gone to her hips. They were pressing her against the sudden rigidity of his powerful body. Even as she registered his urgent hunger for her, she felt one of his big, lean hands seeking between them for the soft, rounded curve of her breast...

She pulled away from him abruptly, her mouth swollen, her eyes wild. "N-no," she choked.

He tried to pull her back into his arms. "Why not?" he murmured, his eyes on her mouth.

"Curt," she whispered.

"Curt." He spoke the name as if he didn't recognize it. He blinked. He took a deep breath and suddenly realized where they were and what he'd been doing.

He drew in a harsh, deep breath.

"You have to go home," she said huskily.

He stood up straight and stared down his nose at her. "If you will keep throwing yourself into my arms, what do you expect?" he asked outrageously.

She gaped at him.

"It's no use trying to look innocent," he added as he moved back another step. "And don't start taking off your blouse, it won't work."

"I am not...!" she choked, crossing her arms quickly.

He made a rough sound in his throat. "A likely story. Don't follow me home, either, because I lock my doors at night."

She wanted to react to that teasing banter that she'd enjoyed so much before, but she couldn't forget that he'd taken Julie's side against her.

She stared at him coldly. "I won't follow you home. Not while you're spending all your free time defending Julie Merrill, when I'm the one who was insulted."

He froze over. "The way Julie tells it, you started on her first."

"And you believe her, of course. She's beautiful and rich and sophisticated."

"Something no man in his right mind could accuse you

of,'' he shot back. With a cold glare, he turned and went out the door.

He didn't pause to speak to Curt, who was just coming in the front door. He shot him a look bare of courtesy and stormed outside. He was boiling over with emotion, the strongest of which was frustrated desire.

Libby didn't explain anything to her brother, but she knew he wasn't blind or stupid. He didn't ask questions, either. He just hugged her and smiled.

She went to bed feeling totally at sea. How could an argument lead to something so tempestuous that she'd almost passed out at Jordan's feet? And if he really wanted Julie, then how could he kiss Libby with such frustrated desire? And why had he started another fight before he left?

She was still trying to figure out why she hadn't slapped his arrogant face when she fell asleep.

The tension between Jordan and his neighbors was suddenly visible even to onlookers. He never set foot on their place. When he had a barbecue for his ranch hands in April, to celebrate the impressive calf sale he'd held, Curt wasn't invited. When Libby had a small birthday party to mark her twenty-fourth birthday, Jordan wasn't on the guest list. Jacobsville being the small town it was, people noticed.

''Have you and Jordan had some sort of falling out?'' Mr. Kemp asked while his new secretary, a sweet little brunette fresh out of high school named Jessie, was out to lunch.

Libby looked up at him with wide-eyed innocence. ''Falling out?''

''Julie Merrill has been telling people that she and Jordan have marriage plans,'' he said. ''I don't believe it. Her father's in financial hot water and Jordan's rich. Old man Merrill is going to need a lot of support in today's political climate. He made some bad calls on the budget and education and the voters are out to get him."

"So I've heard. They say Calhoun Ballenger's just pulled ahead in the polls."

"He'll win," Kemp replied. "It's no contest. Regardless of Jordan's backing."

"Mr. Kemp, would they really use what happened at Julie's party as a weapon against her father?" she asked carefully.

"Of course they would!" he said shortly. "Even in Jacobs County, dirty laundry has a value. There are other skeletons in that closet, too. Plenty of them. Merrill has already lost the election. His way of doing business, under the table, is obsolete. He's trying to make Cash Grier fire those arresting officers and swear they lied. It won't happen. He and his daughter just don't know it and she refuses to face defeat."

"She's at Jordan's house every day now," she said on a sigh that was more wistful than she knew. "She's very beautiful."

"She's a tarantula," Kemp said coldly. "She's got her finger in a pie I can't tell you about, but it's about to hit the tabloids. When it does, her father can kiss his career goodbye."

"Sir?"

He lifted both eyebrows. "Can you keep a secret?"

"If I can't, why am I working for you?" she asked pertly.

"Those two officers Grier's backing, who caught the senator driving drunk—" he said. "They've also been investigating a house out on the Victoria road where drugs are bought and sold. That's the real reason they're facing dismissal. Merrill's nephew is our mayor."

"And he's in it up to his neck, I guess?" she fished.

He nodded. "The nephew and Miss Merrill herself. That's where her new Porsche came from."

Libby whistled. "But if Jordan's connected with her..." she said worriedly.

"That's right," he replied. "He'll be right in hot water with her, even though he's not doing anything illegal. Mud not only sticks, it rubs off."

She chewed her lower lip. "You couldn't warn him, I guess?"

He shook his head. "We aren't speaking."

She stared at him. "But you're friends."

"Not anymore. You see, he thinks I took your side unjustly against Miss Merrill."

She frowned. "I'm sorry."

He chuckled. "It will all blow over in a few weeks. You'll see."

She wasn't so confident. She didn't think it would and she hated the thought of seeing Jordan connected with such an unsavory business.

She walked down to Barbara's Café for lunch and ran right into Julie Merrill and Jordan Powell, who were waiting in line together.

"Oh, look, it's the little secretary," Julie drawled when she saw Libby in line behind them. "Still telling lies about me, Miss Collins?" she asked with a laugh.

Jordan was looking at Libby with an expression that was hard to classify.

Libby ignored her, turning instead to speak to one of the girls from the county clerk's office, who was in line behind her.

"Don't you turn your back on me, you little creep!" Julie raged, attracting attention as she walked right up to Libby. Her eyes were glazed, furious. "You told Jordan that I tried to throw my weight around in Kemp's office and it was a lie! You were just trying to make yourself look good, weren't you?!"

Libby felt sick at her stomach. She was no good at dealing with angry people, despite the fact that she had to watch

Kemp's secretaries do it every day. She wasn't really afraid of the other girl, but she was keenly aware of their differences on the social ladder. Julie was rich and well-known and sophisticated. Libby was little more than a rancher's daughter turned legal apprentice.

"Jordan can't stand you, in case you wondered, so it's no use calling him up all the time for help, and standing at his door trying to make him notice you!" Julie continued haughtily. "He wouldn't demean himself by going out with a dirty little nobody like you!"

Libby pulled herself up and stared at the older girl, keenly aware of curious eyes watching and people listening in the crowded lunch traffic. "Jordan is our neighbor, Miss Merrill," she said in a strained tone. Her legs were shaking, but she didn't let it show. "Nothing more. I don't want Jordan."

"Good. I'm glad you realize that Jordan's nothing more than a neighbor, because you're a nuisance! No man in his right mind would look at you twice!"

"Oh, I don't know about that," Harley Fowler said suddenly, moving up the line to look down at Julie Merrill with cold eyes. "I'd say her manners are a damned sight better than yours and your mouth wouldn't get you into any decent man's house in Jacobsville!"

Julie's mouth fell open.

"I wouldn't have her on toast!" one of the Tremaynes' cowboys ventured from his table.

"Hey, Julie, how about a dime bag?" some anonymous voice called. "I need a fix!"

Julie went pale. "Who said that?!" she demanded shakily.

"Julie, let's go," Jordan said curtly, taking her by the arm.

"I'm hungry!" she protested, fighting his hold.

Libby didn't look up as he passed her with Julie firmly at his side. He didn't look at her, either, and his face was white with rage.

As she went out the door, there was a skirl of belligerent

applause from the patrons of the café. Julie made a rude gesture toward them, which was followed by equally rude laughter.

"Isn't she a pain?" The girl from the clerk's office laughed. "Honestly, Libby, you were such a lady! I'd have laid a chair across her thick skull!"

"Me, too," said another girl. "Nobody can stand her. She thinks she's such a debutante."

Libby listened to the talk with a raging heartbeat. She was sick to her stomach from the unexpected confrontation and glad that Jordan had gotten the girl out of the room before things got ugly. But it ruined her lunch. It ruined her whole day.

It didn't occur to Libby that Jordan would be upset about the things that Julie had said in the café, especially since he hadn't said a word to Libby at the time. But he actually came by Kemp's office the next day, hat in hand, to apologize for Julie's behavior.

He looked disappointed when Kemp was sitting perched on the edge of Libby's desk, as if he'd hoped to find her alone. But he recovered quickly.

He gave Kemp a quick glare, his gaze returning at once to Libby. "I wanted to apologize for Julie," he said curtly. "She's sorry she caused a scene yesterday. She's been upset about her father facing drunk-driving charges."

"I don't receive absentee apologies," Libby said coldly. "And you'll never convince me that she *would* apologize."

Kemp's eyebrows collided. "What's that?"

"Julie made some harsh remarks about me in Barbara's Café yesterday," Libby told him, "in front of half the town."

"Why didn't you come and get me?" Kemp asked. "I'd have settled her hash for her," he added, with a dangerous look at Jordan.

"Harley Fowler defended me," Libby said with a quiet

smile. "So did several other gentlemen in the crowd," she added deliberately.

"She's not as bad as you think she is," Jordan said grimly.

"The hell she's not," Kemp replied softly. He got up. "I know things about her that you're going to wish you did and very soon. Libby, don't be long. We've got a case first thing tomorrow. I'll need those notes," he added, nodding toward the computer screen. He went to his office and closed the door.

"What was Kemp talking about?" Jordan asked Libby curiously.

"I could tell you, but you wouldn't believe me," she said sadly, remembering how warm their relationship had been before Julie Merrill clouded the horizon.

He drew in a long breath and moved a little closer, pushing his hat back over his dark hair. He looked down at her with barely contained hunger. Mabel was busy in the back with the photocopier and the girl who was filling in for Violet had gone to a dental appointment. Mr. Kemp was shut up in his office. Libby kept hoping the phone would ring, or someone would come in the front door and save her from Jordan. It was all she could do not to throw herself into his arms, even after the fights they'd had. She couldn't stop being attracted to him.

"Look," he said quietly, "I'm not trying to make an enemy of you. I like Julie. Her father is a good man and he's had some hard knocks lately. They really need my help, Libby. They haven't got anybody else."

She could just imagine Julie crying prettily, lavishing praise on Jordan for being so useful, dressing up in her best—which was considerably better than Libby's best—and making a play for him. She might be snippy and aggressive toward other women, but Julie Merrill was a practiced seducer. She knew how to wind men around her finger. She was young and beautiful and cultured and rich.

She knew tricks that most men—even Jordan—wouldn't be able to resist.

"Why are you so attracted to her?" Libby wondered aloud.

Jordan gave her an enigmatic look. "She's mature," he said without thinking. "She knows exactly what she wants and she goes after it wholeheartedly. Besides that, she's a woman who could have anybody."

"And she wants you," she said for him.

He shrugged. "Yes. She does."

She studied his lean, hard face, surprising a curious rigidity there before he concealed it. "I suppose you're flattered," she murmured.

"She draws every man's eye when she walks into a room," he said slowly. "She can play the piano like a professional. She speaks three languages. She's been around the world several times. She's dated some of the most famous actors in Hollywood. She's even been presented to the queen in England." He sighed. "Most men would have a hard time turning up their noses at a woman like that."

"In other words, she's like a trophy."

He studied her arrogantly. "You could say that. But there's something more, too. She needs me. She said everyone in town had turned their backs on her father. Calhoun Ballenger is drawing financial support from some of the richest families in town, the same people who promised Senator Merrill their support and then withdrew it. Julie was in tears when she told me how he'd been sold out by his best friends. Until I came along, he actually considered dropping out of the race."

And pigs fly, Libby thought privately, but she didn't say it. The Merrills were dangling their celebrity in front of Jordan, a man who'd been shut out of high society even though he was now filthy rich. They were offering him entry into a closed community. All that and beautiful Julie as well.

''Did you hear what she said to me in Barbara's Café?''
she wondered aloud.

''What do you mean?'' he asked curiously.

''You stood there and let her attack me, without saying
a word.''

He scowled. ''I was talking to Brad Henry while we
stood in line, about a bull he wanted to sell. I didn't realize
what was going on until Julie raised her voice. By then,
Harley Fowler and several other men were making catcalls
at her. I thought the best thing to do would be to get her
outside before things escalated.''

''Did you hear her accuse me of chasing you? Did you
hear her warn me off you?''

He cocked his head. ''I heard that part,'' he admitted.
''She's very possessive and more jealous of me than I realized. But I didn't like having her insult you, if that's what
you mean,'' he said quietly. ''I told her so later. She said
she'd apologize, but I thought it might come easier from
me. She's insecure, Libby. You wouldn't think so, but she
really takes things to heart.''

A revelation a minute, Libby was thinking. Jordan actually believed what he was saying. Julie had really done
a job on him.

''She said that you wouldn't waste your time on a nobody like me,'' she persisted.

''Women say things they don't mean all the time.'' He
shrugged it off. ''You take things to heart, too, Libby,'' he
added gently. ''You're still very young.''

''You keep saying that,'' she replied, exasperated. ''How
old do I have to be for you to think of me as an adult?''

He moved closer, one lean hand going to her slender
throat, slowly caressing it. ''I've thought of you like that
for a long time,'' he said deeply. ''But you're an addiction
I can't afford. You said it yourself—you're ambitious. You
won't be satisfied in a small town. Like the old-timers used
to say, you want to go and see the elephant.''

She was caught in his dark eyes, spellbound. She'd said

that, yes, because of the way he'd behaved about Julie's insults. She'd wanted to sting him. But she didn't mean it. She wasn't ambitious. All she wanted was Jordan. Her eyes were lost in his.

"The elephant?" she parroted, her gaze on his hard mouth.

"You want to see the world," he translated. But he was moving closer as he said it and his head was bending, even against his will. This was stupid. He couldn't afford to let himself be drawn into this sweet trap. Libby wanted a career. She was young and ambitious. He'd go in headfirst and she'd take off and leave him, just as Duke Wright's young wife had left him in search of fame and fortune. He'd deliberately drawn back from Libby and let himself be vamped by Julie Merrill, to show this little firecracker that he hadn't been serious about those kisses they'd exchanged. He wasn't going to risk his heart on a gamble this big. Libby was in love with love. She was attracted to him. But that wasn't love. She was too young to know the difference. He wasn't. He'd grabbed at Julie the way a drowning man reaches for a life jacket. Libby didn't know that. He couldn't admit it.

While he was thinking, he was parting her lips with his. He forgot where they were, who they were. He forgot the arguments and all the reasons he shouldn't do this.

"Libby," he growled against her soft lips.

She barely heard him. Her blood was singing in her veins like a throbbing chorus. Her arms went around his neck in a stranglehold. She pushed up against him, forcing into his mouth in urgency.

His arms swallowed her up whole. The kiss was slow, deep, hungry. It was invasive. Her whole body began to throb with delight. It began to swell. Their earlier kisses had been almost chaste. These were erotic. They were... narcotic.

A soft little cry of pleasure went from her mouth into

his and managed to penetrate the fog of desire she was drowning him in.

He jerked back from her as if he'd been stung. He fought to keep his inner turmoil from showing, his weakness from being visible to her. His big hands caught her waist and pushed her firmly away.

"I know," she said breathlessly. "You think I've had snakebite on my lip and you were only trying to draw out the poison."

He burst out laughing in spite of himself.

She swallowed hard and backed away another step. "Just think how Julie Merrill would react if she saw you kissing me."

That wiped the smile off his face. "That wasn't a kiss," he said.

"No kidding?" She touched her swollen mouth ironically. "I'll bet Julie could even give you lessons."

"Don't talk about her like that," he warned.

"You think she's honest and forthright, because you are," she said, a little breathless. "You're forgetting that her father is a career politician. They both know how to bend the truth without breaking it, how to influence public opinion."

"Politics is a science," he retorted.

"It can be a horrible corruption, as well," she reminded him. "Calhoun Ballenger has taken a lot of heat from them, even a sexual harassment charge that had no basis in fact. Fortunately, people around here know better, and it backfired. It only made Senator Merrill look bad."

His eyes began to glitter. "That wasn't fiction. The woman swore it happened."

"She was one of Julie's cousins," she said with disgust.

He looked as if he hadn't known that. He scowled, but he didn't answer her.

"Julie thinks my brother and I are so far beneath her that we aren't even worth mentioning," she continued, folding her arms over her chest. "She chooses her friends by their social status and bank accounts. Curt and I are losers in her book and she doesn't think we're fit to associate with you. She'll find a way to push you right out of our lives.''

''I don't have social status, but I'm welcome in their home,'' he said flatly.

''There's an election coming up, they don't have enough money to win it, but you do. They'll take your money and make you feel like an equal until you're not needed anymore. Then you'll be out on your ear. You don't come from old money, Jordan, even if you're rich now…''

''You don't know a damned thing about what I come from,'' he snapped.

The furious statement caught her off guard. She knew Jordan had made his own fortune, but he never spoke about his childhood. His mother worked as a housekeeper. Everybody knew it. He sounded as if he couldn't bear to admit his people were only laborers.

''I didn't mean to be insulting,'' she began slowly.

''Hell! You're doing your best to turn me against Julie. She said you would,'' he added. ''She said something else, too—that you're involved with Harley Fowler.''

She refused to react to that. ''Harley's sweet. He defended me when Julie was insulting me.''

That was a sore spot, because Jordan hadn't really heard what Julie was saying until it was too late. He didn't like Harley, anyway.

''Harley's a nobody.''

''Just like me,'' she retorted. ''I'd much rather have Harley than you, Jordan,'' she added. ''He may be just a working stiff, but he's got more class than you'll ever have, even if you hang out with the Merrills for the next fifty years!''

That did it. He gave her a furious glare, spit out a word that would have insulted Satan himself and marched right out the door.

''And stay out!'' she called after it slammed.

Kemp stuck his head out of his office door and stared at

her. "Are you that same shy, introverted girl who came to work here last year?"

She grinned at him through her heartbreak. "You're rubbing off on me, Mr. Kemp," she remarked.

He laughed curtly and went back into his office.

Later, Libby was miserable. They'd exhumed her father's body and taken it up to the state crime lab in Austin for tests.

Curt was furious when she told him that Jordan had been to her office to apologize for the Merrill girl.

"As if she'd ever apologize to the likes of us," he said angrily. "And Jordan just stood by and let her insult you in the café without saying a word!"

She gaped at him. "How did you know that?"

"Harley Fowler came by where I was working this morning to tell me about it. He figured, rightly, that you'd try to keep it to yourself." He sank down into a chair. "I gave Jordan notice this afternoon. In two weeks, I'm out of there."

She grimaced. "But, Curt, where will you go?"

"Right over to Duke Wright's place," he replied with a smile. "I already lined up a job and I'll get a raise, to boot."

"That's great," she said, and meant it.

"We'll be fine. Don't worry about it." He sighed. "It's so much lately, isn't it, Sis? But we'll survive. We will!"

"I know that, Curt. I'm not worried."

But she was. She hated being enemies with Jordan, who was basically a kind and generous man. She was furious with the Merrills for coming between them for such a selfish reason. They only wanted Jordan's money for the old man's reelection campaign. They didn't care about Jordan. But perhaps he was flattered to be included in such high

society, to be asked to hang out with their friends and ac-
quaintances.

But Libby knew something about the people the Merrills
associated with that, perhaps, Jordan didn't. Many of them
were addicts, either to liquor or drugs. They did nothing
for the community; only for themselves. They wanted to
know the right people, be seen in the right places, have
money that showed when people looked. But to Libby, who
loved her little house and little ranch, it seemed terribly
artificial.

She didn't have much but she was happy with her life.
She enjoyed planting things and watching them grow. She
liked teaching Vacation Bible School in the summer and
working in the church nursery with little children. She liked
cooking food to carry to bereaved families when relatives
died. She liked helping out with church bazaars, donating
time to the local soup kitchen. She didn't put on airs, but
people seemed to like her just the way she was.

Certainly Harley Fowler did. He'd come over to see her
the day after Julie's attack in the café, to make sure she
was all right. He'd asked her out to eat the following Saturday night.

"Only to Shea's," he chuckled. "I just paid off a new
transmission for my truck and I'm broke."

She'd grinned at him. "That's okay. I'm broke, too!"

He shook his head, his eyes sparkling as he looked down
at her with appreciation. "Libby, you're my kind of people."

"Thanks, Harley."

"Say, can you dance?"

She blinked. "Well, I can do a two-step."

"That's good enough." He chuckled. "I've been taking
these dance courses on the side."

"I know. I heard about the famous waltz with Janie
Brewster at the Cattleman's Ball last year."

He smiled sheepishly. "Well, now I'm working on the

jitterbug and I hear that Shea's live band can play that sort of thing.''

"You can teach me to jitterbug, Harley," she agreed at once. "I'd love to go dancing with you."

He looked odd. "Really?"

She nodded and smiled. "Really."

"Then I'll see you Saturday about six. We can eat there, too."

"Suits me. I'll leave supper for Curt in the refrigerator. That was really nice of you to go to bat for him with your boss, Harley," she added seriously. "Thanks."

He shrugged. "Mr. Parks wasn't too pleased with the way Powell's sucking up to the Merrills, either," he said. "He knows things about them."

"So do I," she replied. "But Jordan doesn't take well-meant advice."

"His problem," Harley said sharply.

She nodded. "Yes, Harley. It's his problem. I'll see you Saturday!" she added, laughing.

When she told Curt about the upcoming date, he seemed pleased. "It's about time you went out and had some fun for a change."

"I like Harley a lot," she told her brother.

He searched her eyes knowingly. "But he's not Jordan."

She turned away. "Jordan made his choice. I'm making mine." She smiled philosophically. "I dare say we'll both be happy!"

Chapter Six

Libby and Harley raised eyebrows at Shea's Roadhouse and Bar with their impromptu rendition of the jitterbug. It was a full house, too, on a Saturday night. At least two of the Tremayne brothers were there with their wives, and Calhoun Ballenger and his wife, Abby, were sitting at a table nearby with Leo Hart and his wife, Janie.

"I'm absolutely sure that Calhoun's going to win the state senate seat," Harley said in Libby's ear when they were seated again, drinking iced tea and eating hamburgers. "It looks like he's going to get some support from the Harts."

"Is Mr. Parks in his corner, too?" she asked.

He nodded. "All the way. The political landscape has been changing steadily for the past few years, but old man Merrill just keeps going with his old agenda. He hasn't got a clue what the voters want anymore. And, more important, he doesn't control them through his powerful friends."

"You'd think his daughter would be forward-thinking," she pointed out.

He didn't say anything. But his face was eloquent.

"Somebody said she was thinking of running for public office in Jacobsville," she began.

"No name identification," Harley said at once. "You have to have it to win an office. Without it, all the money in the world won't get you elected."

"You seem to know something about politics," she commented.

He averted his eyes. "Do I?" he mused.

Harley never talked about his family, or his past. He'd shown up at Cy Parks' place one day and proved himself to be an exceptional cowboy, but nobody knew much about him. He'd gone on a gigantic drug bust with Jacobsville's ex-mercenaries and he had a reputation for being a tough customer. But he was as mysterious in his way as the town's police chief, Cash Grier.

"Wouldn't you just know they'd show up and spoil everything?" Harley said suddenly, glaring toward the door.

Sure enough, there was Jordan Powell in an expensive Western-cut sports coat and Stetson and boots, escorting pretty Julie Merrill in a blue silk dress that looked simple and probably cost the earth.

"Doesn't she look expensive?" Harley mused.

"She probably is," Libby said, trying not to look and sound as hurt as she really was. It killed her to see Jordan there with that terrible woman.

"She's going to find out, pretty soon, that she's the equivalent of three-day-old fish with this crowd," Harley predicted coolly, watching her stick her nose up at the Ballengers as she passed them.

"I just hope she doesn't drag Jordan down with her," Libby said softly. "He started out like us, Harley," she added. "He was just a working cowboy with ambition."

Jordan seated Julie and shot a cool glance in Harley and Libby's direction, without even acknowledging them. He sat down, placing his Stetson on a vacant chair and motioned a waiter.

"Did you want something stronger to drink?" Harley asked her.

She grinned at him. "I don't have a head for liquor, Harley. I'd rather stick to iced tea, if you don't mind."

"So would I," he confided, motioning for a waiter.

The waiter, with a fine sense of irony, walked right past Jordan to take Harley's order. Julie Merrill was sputtering like a stepped-on garden hose.

"Two more iced teas, Charlie," Harley told the waiter. "And thanks for giving us preference."

"Oh, I know who the best people are, Harley," the boy said with a wicked grin. And he walked right past Jordan and Julie again, without even looking at them. A minute later, Jordan got up and stalked over to the counter to order their drinks.

"He'll smolder for the rest of the night over that," Harley mused. "So will she, unless I miss my guess. Isn't it amazing," he added thoughtfully, "that a man with as much sense as Jordan Powell can't see right through that debutante?"

"How is it that you can?" Libby asked him curiously.

He shrugged. "I know politicians all too well," he said, and for a moment, his expression was distant. "Old man Merrill has been hitting the bottle pretty hard lately," he said. "It isn't going to sit well with his constituents that he got pulled over and charged with drunk driving by Jacobsville's finest."

"Do you think they'll convict him?" she wondered aloud.

"You can bet money on it," Harley replied. "The world has shifted ten degrees. Local politicians don't meet in parked cars and make policy anymore. The sunshine laws mean that the media get wind of anything crooked and they report it. Senator Merrill has been living in the past. He's going to get a hell of a wake-up call at the primary election, when Calhoun Ballenger knocks him off the Democratic ballot as a contender."

"Mr. Ballenger looks like a gentleman," Libby commented, noticing the closeness of Calhoun and his brunette wife Abby. "He and his wife have been married a long time, haven't they?"

"Years," Harley said. "He and Justin are honest and hardworking men. They came up from nothing, too, although Justin's wife Shelby was a Jacobs before she married him," he reminded her. "A direct descendant of Big John Jacobs. But don't you think either of the Ballenger brothers would have been taken in by Julie Merrill, even when they were still single."

She paused to thank the waiter, who brought their two glasses of tall, cold iced tea. Jordan was still waiting for his order at the counter, while Julie glared at Libby and Harley.

"She's not quite normal, is she?" Libby said quietly. "I mean, that outburst in Barbara's Café was so…violent."

"People on drugs usually are violent," Harley replied. "And irrational." He looked right into Libby's eyes. "She's involved in some pretty nasty stuff, Libby. I can't tell you what I know, but Jordan is damaging himself just by being seen in public with her. The campaigns will get hot and heavy later this month and some dirty linen is about to be exposed to God and the general public."

Libby was concerned. "Jordan's a good man," she said quietly, her eyes going like homing pigeons to his lean, handsome face.

He caught her looking at him and glared. Julie, seeing his attention diverted, looked, too.

Once he returned to the table Julie leaned over and whispered something to Jordan that made him give Libby a killing glare before he started ignoring her completely.

"Watch your back," Harley told Libby as he sipped his iced tea. "She considers you a danger to her plans with Jordan. She'll sell you down the river if she can."

She sighed miserably. "First my stepmother, now Julie,"

she murmured. "I feel like I've got a target painted on my forehead."

"We all have bad times," Harley told her gently, and slid a big hand over one of hers where it lay on the table. "We get through them."

"You, too?" she wondered aloud.

"Yeah. Me, too," he replied, and he smiled at her.

Neither of them saw the furious look on Jordan Powell's face, or the calculating look on Julie's.

The following week, when Libby went to Barbara's Café for lunch, she walked right into Jordan Powell on the sidewalk. He was alone, as she was, and his expression made her feel cold all over.

"What's this about you going up to San Antonio for the night with Harley last Wednesday?" he asked bluntly.

Libby couldn't even formulate a reply for the shock. She'd driven Curt over to Duke Wright's place early Wednesday afternoon and from there she'd driven up to San Antonio to obtain some legal documents from the county clerk's office for Mr. Kemp. She hadn't even seen Harley there.

"I thought you were pure as the driven snow," Jordan continued icily. His dark eyes narrowed on her shocked face. "You put on a good act, don't you, Libby? I don't need to be a mind-reader to know why, either. I'm rich and you and your brother are about to lose your ranch."

"Janet hasn't started probate yet," she faltered.

"That's not what I hear."

"I don't care what you hear," she told him flatly. "Neither Curt nor I care very much what you think, either, Jordan. But you're going to run into serious problems if you hang out with Julie Merrill until her father loses the election."

He glared down at her. "He isn't going to lose," he assured her.

She hated seeing him be so stubborn, especially when

she had at least some idea of what Julie was going to drag him down into. She moved a step closer, her green eyes soft and beseeching. "Jordan, you're an intelligent man," she began slowly. "Surely you can see what Julie wants you for…"

A worldly look narrowed his eyes as they searched over her figure without any reaction at all. "Julie wants me, all right," he replied, coolly. "That's what's driving you to make these wild comments, isn't it? You're jealous because I'm spending so much time with her."

She didn't dare let on what she was feeling. She forced a careless smile. "Am I? You think I don't know when a man is teasing me?"

"You know more than I ever gave you credit for and that's the truth," he said flatly. "You and Harley Fowler." He made it sound like an insult.

"Harley is a fine man," she said, defending him.

"Obviously you think so, or you wouldn't be shacking up with him," he accused. "Does your brother know?"

"I'm a big girl now," she said, furious at the insinuation.

"Both of you had better remember that I make a bad enemy," he told her. "Whatever happens with your ranch, I don't want to have a subdivision full of people on my border."

He didn't know that Libby and Curt had already discussed how they were going to manage without their father's life insurance policy to pay the mortgage payments that were still owed. Riddle had taken out a mortgage on the ranch to buy Janet's Mercedes. Janet had waltzed off with the money and the private detective Jordan had recommended to Mr. Kemp had drawn a blank when he tried to dig into Janet's past. The will hadn't been probated, either, so there was no way Riddle Curtis's children could claim any of their inheritance with which to pay bills or make that huge mortgage payment. They'd had to let their only helper—their part-time cowboy—go, for lack of funds to pay him. They only had one horse left and they'd had to sell off most of their cattle. The only money coming in right now was what Curt and Libby earned in their respective jobs, and it wasn't much.

Of course, Libby wasn't going to share that information with a hostile Jordan Powell. Things were so bad that she and Curt might have to move off the ranch anyway because they couldn't make that mortgage payment at the end of the month. It was over eight hundred dollars. Their collective take-home pay wouldn't amount to that much and there were still other bills owing. Janet had run up huge bills while Riddle was still alive.

Jordan felt sick at what he was saying to Libby. He was jealous of Harley Fowler, furiously jealous. He couldn't bear the thought of Libby in bed with the other man. She wasn't even denying what Julie had assured him had happened between them. Libby, in Harley's arms, kissing him with such hunger that his toes tingled. Libby, loving Harley...

Jordan ached to have her for himself. He dreamed of her every night. But Libby was with Harley now. He'd lost his chance. He couldn't bear it!

"Is Harley going to loan you enough money to keep the ranch going until Janet's found?" he wondered aloud. He smiled coldly. "He hasn't got two dimes to rub together, from what I hear."

Libby remembered the mortgage payments she couldn't make. Once, she might have bent her pride enough to ask Jordan to loan it to her. Not anymore. Not after what he'd said to her.

She lifted her chin. "That's not your business, Jordan," she said proudly.

"Don't expect me to lend it to you," he said for spite.

"Jordan, I wouldn't ask you for a loan if the house burned down," she assured him, unflinching. "Now, if you'll excuse me, I'm using up my lunch hour."

She started to go around him, but he caught her arm and marched her down the little alley between her office and the town square. It was an alcove, away from traffic, with no prying eyes.

While she was wondering what was on his mind, he backed her up against the cold brick and brought his mouth down on her lips.

She pushed at his chest, but he only gave her his weight, pressing her harder into the wall. His own body was almost as hard, especially when his hips shifted suddenly, and lowered squarely against her own. She shivered at the slow caress of his hands on her ribcage while the kiss went on and on. She couldn't breathe. She didn't want to breathe. Her body ached for something more than this warm, heady torment. She moaned huskily under the hard, furious press of his mouth.

He lifted his head a bare inch and looked into her wide green eyes with possession and desire. It never stopped. He couldn't get within arm's length of her without giving in to temptation. Did she realize? No. She had no idea. She thought it was a punishment for her harsh words. It was more. It was anguish.

"You still want me," he ground out. "Do you think I don't know?"

"What?" she murmured, her eyes on his mouth. She could barely think at all. She felt his body so close that when he breathed, her chest deflated. Her breasts ached at the warm pressure of his broad chest. It was heaven to be so close to him. And she didn't dare let it show.

"Are you trying to prove something?" she murmured, forcing her hands to push instead of pull at his shoulders.

"Only that Harley isn't in my league," he said in a husky, arrogant tone, as he bent again and forced her mouth open under the slow, exquisite skill of his kisses. "In fact," he bit off against her lips, "neither are you, cupcake."

She wanted to come back with some snappy reply. She really did. But the sensations he was arousing were hypnotic, drugging. She felt him move one long, powerful jean-clad leg in between both of hers. It was broad daylight, in the middle of town. He was making love to her against a wall. And she didn't care.

She moved against him, her lips welcoming, her hands spreading, caressing, against his ribcage, his chest. There was no tomorrow. There was only Jordan, wanting her.

Her body throbbed in time with her frantic heartbeat. She was hot all over, swelling, aching. She wanted relief. Anything…!

Voices coming close pushed them apart when she would have said that nothing could. Jordan stepped back, his face a rigid mask. She looked up at him, her crushed mouth red from the ardent pressure, her eyes soft and misty and dazed.

Her pocketbook was on the ground. He reached down and handed it back to her, watching as she put the strap over her shoulder and stared up at him, still bemused.

She wanted to tell him that Harley was a better lover, to make some flip remark that would sting him. But she couldn't.

He was in pretty much the same shape. He hated the very thought of Harley. But even through the jealousy, he realized that Libby's responses weren't those of any experienced woman. When Julie kissed him, it was with her whole body. She was more than willing to do anything he liked. But he couldn't take Julie to bed because he didn't want her that way. It was a source of irritation and amazement to him. And to Julie, who made sarcastic remarks about his prowess.

It wasn't a lack of ability. It was just a lack of desire. But he raged with it when he looked at Libby. He'd never wanted a woman to the point of madness until now and she was the one woman he couldn't have.

"Women and their damned ambitions," he said under his breath. "Damn Harley. And damn you, Libby!"

"Damn you, too, Jordan," she said breathlessly. "And don't expect me to drag you into any more alleys and make love to you, if that's going to be your attitude!"

She turned and walked away before he had time to realize what she'd said. He had to bite back a laugh. This was no laughing matter. He had to get a grip on himself before Libby realized what was wrong with him.

After their disturbing encounter, she wondered if she and Curt wouldn't do better to just move off their property and live somewhere else. In fact, she told herself, that might not be a bad idea.

Mr. Kemp didn't agree.

"You have to maintain a presence on the property," he told Libby firmly. "If you move out, Janet might use that against you in court."

"You don't understand," she groaned. "Jordan is driving me crazy. And every time I look out the window, Julie's speeding down the road to Jordan's house."

"Jordan's being conned," he ventured.

"I know that, but he won't listen," Libby said, sitting down heavily behind her desk. "Julie's got him convinced that I'm running wild with Harley Fowler."

"That woman is big trouble," he said. "I'd give a lot to see her forced to admit what she did to the Culbertson girl at that party."

"You think it was her?" she asked, shocked.

He shrugged. "Nobody else had a motive," he said, his eyes narrow and cold. "Shannon Culbertson was running against her for class president and Julie wanted to win. I don't think she planned to kill her. She was going to set her up with one of the boys she was dating and ruin Shannon's reputation. But it backfired. At least, that's my theory. If this gets out it's going to disgrace her father even further."

"Isn't he already disgraced enough because of the drunk-driving charges?" she asked.

"He and his cronies at city hall are trying desperately to get those charges dropped, before they get into some newspaper whose publisher doesn't owe him a favor," Kemp replied, perching on the edge of her desk. "There's a disciplinary hearing at city hall next month for the officers involved. Grier says the council is going to try to have the police officers fired.''

She smiled. ''I can just see Chief Grier letting that happen.''

Kemp chuckled. ''I think the city council is going to be in for a big surprise. Our former police chief, Chet Blake, never would buck the council, or stand up for any officer who did something politically incorrect with the city fathers. Grier isn't like his cousin.''

''What if they fire him, too?'' she asked.

He stood up. ''If they even try, there will be a recall of the city council and the mayor,'' Kemp said simply. ''I can almost guarantee it. A lot of people locally are fed up with city management. Solid waste is backing up, there's no provision for water conservation, the fire department hasn't got one piece of modern equipment, and we're losing revenue hand over fist because nobody wants to mention raising taxes.''

''I didn't realize that.''

''Grier did.'' He smiled to himself. ''He's going to shake up this town. It won't be a bad thing, either.''

''Do you think he'll stay?''

Kemp nodded. ''He's put down deep roots already, although I don't think he realizes how deep they go just yet.''

Like everyone else in Jacobsville, Libby knew what was going on in Cash Grier's private life. After all, it had been in most of the tabloids. Exactly what the situation was between him and his houseguest, Tippy Moore, was anybody's guess. The couple were equally tight-lipped in public.

''Could I ask you to do something for me, sir?'' she asked suddenly.

''Of course.''

''Could you find out if they've learned anything about… Daddy at the state crime lab and how much longer it's going to be before they have a report?'' she asked.

He frowned. "Good Lord, I didn't realize how long it had been since the exhumation," he said. "Certainly. I'll get right on it, in fact."

"Thanks," she said.

He shrugged. "No problem." He got to his feet and hesitated. "Have you talked to Violet lately?" he asked reluctantly.

"She's lost weight and she's having her hair frosted," she began.

His lips made a thin line. "I don't want to know about her appearance. I only wondered how she likes her new job."

"A lot," she replied. She pursed her lips. "In fact, she and my brother are going out on a date Saturday night."

"Your brother knows her?" he asked.

She nodded. "He's working for Duke Wright, too..."

"Since when?" he exclaimed. "He was Jordan's right-hand man!"

She averted her eyes. "Not anymore. Jordan said some pretty bad things about me and Curt quit."

Kemp cursed. "I don't understand how a man who was so concerned for both of you has suddenly become an enemy. However," he added, "I imagine Julie Merrill has something to do with his change of heart."

"He's crazy about her, from what we hear."

"He's crazy, all right," he said, turning back toward his office. "He'll go right down the tubes with her and her father if he isn't careful."

"I tried to tell him. He accused me of being jealous."

He glanced back at her. "And you aren't?" he probed softly.

Her face closed up. "What good would it do, Mr. Kemp? Either people like you or they don't."

Kemp had thought, privately, that it was more than liking on Jordan's part. But apparently, he'd been wrong right down the line.

"Bring your pad, if you don't mind, Libby," he said. "I

want you to look up a case for me at the courthouse law library.''

"Yes, sir," she said, picking up her pad. It was always better to stay busy. That way she didn't have so much time to think.

She was walking into the courthouse when she met Calhoun Ballenger coming out of it. He stopped and grinned at her.

"Just the woman I was looking for," he said. "On the assumption that I win this primary election for the Democratic candidate, how would you like to join my campaign staff in your spare time?"

She caught her breath. "Mr. Ballenger, I'm very flattered!"

"Duke Wright tells me that you have some formidable language skills," he continued. "Not that my secretaries don't, but they've got their hands full right now trying to get people to go to the polls and vote for me in May. I need someone to write publicity for me. Are you interested?"

"You bet!" she said at once.

"Great! Come by the ranch Saturday about one. I've invited a few other people as well."

"Not...the Merrills or Jordan Powell?" she asked worriedly.

He glowered at her. "I do not invite the political competition to staff meetings," he said with mock hauteur. He grinned. "Besides, Jordan and I aren't speaking."

"That's a relief," she said honestly.

"You're on the wrong side of him, too, I gather?"

She nodded. "Me and half the town."

"More than half, if I read the situation right," he said with a sigh. "A handful of very prominent Democrats have changed sides and they're now promoting me." He smiled. "More for our side."

She smiled back. "Exactly! Well, then, I'll see you Saturday."

"I've already invited your boss and Duke Wright, but Duke won't come," he added heavily. "I invited Grier, and Duke's still browned off about the altercation he had with our police chief."

"He shouldn't have swung on him," she pointed out.

"I'm sure he knows that now," he agreed, his eyes twinkling. "See you."

She gave him a wave and walked into the courthouse lobby. Jordan Powell was standing there with a receipt for his automobile tag and glaring daggers at Libby.

"You're on a friendly basis with Calhoun Ballenger, I gather?" he asked.

"I'm going to work on his campaign staff," she replied with a haughty smile.

"He's going to lose," he told her firmly. "He doesn't have name identification."

She smiled at him. "He hasn't been arrested for drunk driving, to my knowledge," she pointed out.

His eyes flashed fire. "That's a frame," he returned. "Grier's officers planted evidence against him."

She glared back. "Chief Grier is honest and openhanded," she told him. "And his officers would never be asked to do any such thing!"

"They'll be out of work after that hearing," he predicted.

"You swallow everything Julie tells you, don't you, Jordan?" she asked quietly. "Maybe you should take a look at the makeup of our city council. Those were people who once owned big businesses in Jacobsville and had tons of money. But their companies are all going downhill and they're short of ready cash. They aren't the people who have the power today. And if you think Chief Grier is going to stand by and let them railroad his employees, you're way off base."

Jordan didn't reply at once. He stared at Libby until her face colored.

"I never thought you'd go against me, after all I've done for you and Curt," he said.

She was thinking the same thing. It made her ashamed to recall how he'd tried to help them both when Janet was first under suspicion of murder and fraud. But he'd behaved differently since he'd gotten mixed up with Senator Merrill's daughter. He'd changed, drastically.

"You have done a lot for us," she had to agree. "We'll always be grateful for it. But you took sides against us first, Jordan. You stood by with your mouth closed in Barbara's Café and let Julie humiliate me."

Jordan's eyes flashed. It almost looked like guilt. "You had enough support."

"Yes, from Harley Fowler. At least someone spoke up for me."

He looked ice cold. "You were rude to Julie first, in your own office."

"Why don't you ask Mr. Kemp who started it?" she replied.

"Kemp hates her," he said bluntly. "He'd back your story. I'm working for Senator Merrill and I'm going to get him reelected. You just side with the troublemakers and do what you please. But don't expect me to come around with my hat in my hand."

"I never did, Jordan," she said calmly. "I'm just a no-body around Jacobsville and I'm very aware of it. I'm not sophisticated or polished or rich, and I have no manners. On the other hand, I have no aspirations to high society, in case you wondered."

"Good thing. You'd never fit in," he bit off.

She smiled sadly. "And you think you will?" she challenged softly. "You may have better table manners than I do—and more money—but your father was poor. None of your new high-class friends is ever going to forget that. Even if you do."

He said something nasty. She colored a little, but she didn't back down.

"Don't worry, I know my place, Mr. Powell," she replied, just to irritate him. "I'm a minor problem that you've put out beside the road. I won't forget."

She was making him feel small. He didn't like it.

"Thank you for being there when we needed you most," she added quietly. "We aren't going to sell our land to developers."

"If you ever get title to it," he said coldly.

She shrugged. "That's out of our hands."

"Kemp will do what he can for you," he said, feeling guilty, because he knew that she and Curt had no money for attorneys. He'd heard that Janet was still missing and that Kemp's private detective had drawn a blank when he looked into her past. Libby and Curt must be worried sick about money.

"Yes, Mr. Kemp will do what he can for us." She studied his face, so hard and uncompromising, and wondered what had happened to make them so distant after the heated promises of those kisses they'd exchanged only weeks before.

"Curt likes working for Wright, I suppose?" he asked reluctantly.

She nodded. "He's very happy there."

"Julie had a cousin who trains horses. He's won trophies in steeplechase competition. He's working in Curt's place now, with my two new thoroughbreds."

"I suppose Julie wants to keep it all in the family," she replied.

He glared down at her. "Keep all what in the family?"

"Your money, Jordan," she said sweetly.

"You wouldn't have turned it down, if I'd given you the chance," he accused sarcastically. "You were laying it on thick."

"Who was kissing whom in the alley?" she returned huskily.

He didn't like remembering that. He jerked his wide-brimmed hat down over his eyes. "A moment of weakness. Shouldn't have happened. I'm not free anymore."

Insinuating that he and Julie were much more than friends, Libby thought correctly. She looked past Jordan to Julie, who was just coming out of the courthouse looking elegant and cold as ice. She saw Libby standing with Jordan and her lips collided furiously.

"Jordan! Let's go!" she called to him angrily.

"I was only passing the time of day with him, Julie," Libby told the older woman with a vacant smile.

"You keep your sticky hands to yourself, you little liar," Julie told her as she passed on the steps. "Jordan is mine!"

"No doubt you mean his money is yours, right?" Libby ventured.

Julie drew back her hand and slapped Libby across the cheek as hard as she could. "Damn you!" she raged.

Libby was shocked at the unexpected physical reply, but she didn't retaliate. She just stood there, straight and dignified, with as much pride as she could muster. Around the two women, several citizens stopped and looked on with keen disapproval.

One of them was Officer Dana Hall, one of the two police officers who had arrested Senator Merrill for drunk driving.

She walked right up to Libby. "That was assault, Miss Collins," she told Libby. "If you want to press charges, I can arrest Miss Merrill on the spot."

"Arrest!" Julie exploded. "You can't arrest me!"

"I most certainly can," Officer Hall replied. "Miss Collins, do you want to press charges?"

Libby stared at Julie Merrill with cold pleasure, wondering how it would look on the front page of Jacobsville's newspaper.

"Wouldn't that put another kink in your father's reelection campaign?" Libby ventured softly.

Julie looked past Libby and suddenly burst into tears.

She threw herself into Jordan Powell's arms. "Oh, Jordan, she's going to have me arrested!"

"No, she's not," Jordan said curtly. He glanced at Libby. "She wouldn't dare."

Libby cocked her head. "I wouldn't?" She glared at him. "Look at my cheek, Jordan."

It was red. There was a very obvious handprint on it.

"She insulted me," Julie wailed. "I had every right to hit her back!"

"She never struck you, Miss Merrill," Officer Hall replied coldly. "Striking another person is against the law, regardless of the provocation."

"I never meant to do it!" Julie wailed. She was sobbing, but there wasn't a speck of moisture under her eyes. "Please, Jordan, don't let them put me in jail!"

Libby and Officer Hall exchanged disgusted looks.

"Men are so damned gullible," Libby remarked with a glare at Jordan, who looked outraged. "All right, Julie, have it your way. But you'd better learn to produce tears as well as broken sobs if you want to convince another *woman* that you're crying."

"Jordan, could we go now?" Julie sobbed. "I'm just sick…!"

"Not half as sick as you'll be when your father loses the election, Julie," Libby drawled sweetly, and walked up the steps with Officer Hall at her side. She didn't even look at Jordan as she went into the courthouse.

Chapter Seven

Calhoun Ballenger's meeting with his volunteer staff was a cheerful riot of surprises. Libby found herself working with women she'd known only by name a few months earlier. Now she was suddenly in the cream of society, but with women who didn't snub her or look down their noses at her social position.

Libby was delighted to find herself working with Violet, who'd come straight from her job at Duke Wright's ranch for the meeting.

"This is great!" Violet exclaimed, hugging Libby. "I've missed working with you!"

"I've missed you, too, Violet," Libby assured her. She shook her head as she looked at the other woman. "You look great!"

Violet grinned. She'd dropped at least two dress sizes. She was well-rounded, but no longer obese even to the most critical eye. She'd had her brown hair frosted and it was waving around her face and shoulders. She was wearing a low-cut dress that emphasized the size of her pretty breasts, and her small waist and voluptuous hips, along with high heels that arched her small feet nicely.

"I've worked hard at the gym," Violet confessed. She was still laughing when her eyes collided with Blake Kemp's across the room. The expression left her face. She averted her eyes quickly. "Excuse me, won't you, Libby? I came with Curt. You, uh, don't mind, do you?" she added worriedly.

"Don't be silly," Libby said with a genuine smile. "Curt's nice. So are you. I think you'd make a lovely couple…"

"Still happy with Duke Wright, Miss Hardy?" came a cold, biting comment from Libby's back.

Blake Kemp moved into view, his pale eyes expressive on Violet's pretty figure and the changes in the way she dressed.

"I'm…very happy with him, Mr. Kemp," Violet said, clasping her hands together tightly. "If you'll excuse me…"

"You've lost weight," Kemp said gruffly.

Violet's eyes widened. "And you actually noticed?"

The muscles in his face tautened. "You look…nice."

Violet's jaw dropped. She was literally at a loss for words. Her eyes lifted to Kemp's and they stood staring at each other for longer than was polite, neither speaking or moving.

Kemp shifted restlessly on his long legs. "How's your mother?"

Violet swallowed hard. "She's not doing very well, I'm afraid. You know…about the exhumation?"

Kemp nodded. "They're still in the process of evaluating Curt and Libby's father's remains, as well, at the crime lab. So far, they have nothing to report."

Violet looked beside him at Libby and winced. "I didn't know, Libby. I'm so sorry."

"So am I, for you," Libby replied. "We didn't want to do it, but we had to know for sure."

"Will they really be able to tell anything, after all this time?" Violet asked Kemp, and she actually moved a step closer to him.

He seemed to catch his breath. He was looking at her oddly. "I assume so." His voice was deeper, too. Involuntarily, his lean fingers reached out and touched Violet's long hair. "I like the frosting," he said reluctantly. "It makes your eyes look...bluer."

"Does it?" Violet asked, but her eyes were staring into his as if she'd found treasure there.

With an amused smile, Libby excused herself and joined her brother, who was talking to the police chief.

Cash Grier noticed her approach and smiled. He looked older somehow and there were new lines around his dark eyes.

"Hi, Chief," she greeted him. "How's it going?"

"Don't ask," Curt chuckled. "He's in the middle of a controversy."

"So are we," Libby replied. "We're on the wrong side of the election and Jordan Powell is furious at us."

"We're on the right side," Cash said carelessly. "The city fathers are in for a rude awakening." He leaned down. "I have friends in high places." He paused. "I also have friends in *low* places." He grinned.

Libby and Curt burst out laughing, because they recognized the lines from a country song they'd all loved.

Calhoun Ballenger joined them, clapping Cash on the back affectionately. "Thanks for coming," he said. "Even if it is putting another nail in your coffin with the mayor."

"They mayor can kiss my..." Cash glanced at Libby and grinned. "Never mind."

They all laughed.

"She's lived with me all her life," Curt remarked. "She's practically unshockable."

"How's Tippy?" Calhoun asked.

Cash smiled. "Doing better, thanks. She'd have come, too, but she's still having a bad time."

"No wonder," Calhoun replied, recalling the ordeal Tippy had been through in the hands of kidnappers. It had been in all the tabloids. "Good thing they caught the culprits who kidnapped her."

"Isn't it?" Cash said, not giving away that he'd caught them, with the help of an old colleague. "Nice turnout, Calhoun," he added, looking around them. "I thought you invited Judd."

"I did," Calhoun said at once, "but the twins have a cold."

"Damn!" Cash grimaced. "I told Judd that he and Crissy needed to stop running that air conditioner all night!"

"It wasn't that," Calhoun confided. "They went to the Coltrains' birthday party for their son—his second birthday—and that's where they got the colds."

Cash sighed. "Poor babies."

"He's their godfather," Calhoun told Libby and Curt. "But he thinks Jessamina belongs to him."

"She does," Cash replied haughtily.

Nobody mentioned what the tabloids had said—that Tippy had been pregnant with Cash's child a few weeks earlier and lost it just before her ordeal with the kidnapping.

Libby diplomatically changed the subject. "Mr. Kemp said that you can put up campaign posters in our office windows," she told Calhoun, "and Barbara's willing to let you put up as many as you like in her café," she added with a grin. "She said she's never going to forgive Julie Merrill for making a scene there."

Calhoun chuckled. "I've had that sort of offer all week," he replied. "Nobody wants Senator Merrill back in office, but the city fathers have thrown their support behind him and he thinks he's unbeatable. What we really need is a change in city government as well. We're on our second mayor in eight months and this one is afraid of his own shadow."

"He's also Senator Merrill's nephew," Curt added.

"Which is why he's trying to make my officers back down on those DWI charges," Cash Grier interposed.

"I'd like see it. Carlos Garcia wouldn't back down from anybody," Calhoun mused. "Or Officer Dana Hall, either."

"Ms. Hall came to my assistance at the courthouse this week," Libby volunteered. "Julie Merrill slapped me. Officer Hall was more than willing to arrest her, if I'd agreed to press charges."

"Good for Dana," Cash returned. "You be careful, Ms. Collins," he added firmly. "That woman has poor impulse control. I wouldn't put it past her to try and run somebody down."

"Neither would I," Curt added worriedly. "She's already told Jordan some furious lies about us and he believes her."

"She can be very convincing," Libby said, not wanting to verbally attack Jordan even now.

"It may get worse now, with all of you backing me," Calhoun told the small group. "I won't have any hard feelings if you want to withdraw your support."

"Do I look like the sort of man who backs away from trouble?" Cash asked lazily, with a grin.

"Speaking of Duke Wright," Libby murmured dryly, "he's throwing his support to Mr. Ballenger, too. But he had, uh, reservations about coming to the meeting."

Cash chuckled. "I don't hold grudges."

"Yes, but he does," Calhoun said on a chuckle. "He'll get over it. He's got some personal problems right now."

"Don't we all?" Cash replied wistfully, and his dark eyes were troubled.

Libby and Curt didn't add their two cents' worth, but they exchanged quiet looks.

The campaign was winding down for the primary, but all the polls gave Calhoun a huge lead over Merrill. Printed materials were ordered, along with buttons, pencils, bumper stickers and keychains. There was enough promotional matter to blanket the town and in the days that followed, Calhoun's supporters did exactly that in Jacobs County and the surrounding area in the state senatorial district that Merrill represented.

Julie Merrill was acting as her father's campaign manager and she was coordinating efforts for promotion with a group of teenagers she'd hired. Some of them were delinquents and there was a rash of vandalisms pertaining to the destruction of Calhoun's campaign posters.

Cash Grier, predictably, went after the culprits and rounded them up. He got one to talk and the newspapers revealed that Miss Merrill had paid the young man to destroy Calhoun's campaign literature. Julie denied it. But the vandalism stopped.

Meanwhile, acting mayor Ben Brady was mounting a fervent defense for Senator Merrill on the drunk-driving charges and trying to make things hot for the two officers. He ordered them suspended and tried to get the city council to back him up.

Cash got wind of it and phoned Simon Hart, the state's attorney general. Simon phoned the city attorney and they had a long talk. Soon afterward, the officers were notified that they could stay on the job until the hearing the following month.

Meanwhile, the state crime lab revealed the results of its report to Blake Kemp. He walked up to Libby's desk while she was on the phone and waited impatiently for her to hang up.

"They can't find any evidence of foul play, Libby," he said at once.

"And if there was any, they would?" she asked quickly.

He nodded. "I'm almost certain of it. The crime lab verified our medical examiner's diagnosis of myocardial infarction. So Janet's off the hook for that one, at least."

Libby sat back with a long sigh and closed her eyes.

"Thank God. I couldn't have lived with it if she'd poisoned Daddy and we never knew."

He nodded. "On the other hand, they hit paydirt with Violet's father," he added.

She sat up straight. "Poison?"

"Yes," he said heavily. "I'm not going to phone her. I'm going over to Duke Wright's place to tell her in person. Then I'll take her home to talk to her mother. She'll need someone with her."

Yes, she would, and Libby was secretly relieved that Kemp was going to be the person. Violet would need a shoulder to cry on.

"I'll phone Curt and tell him," she said.

"Libby, give me half an hour first," he asked quietly. "I don't want him to tell Violet."

She wondered why, but she wasn't going to pry. "Okay."

He managed a brief smile. "Thanks."

"What about Janet?" she wondered miserably. "They still haven't found her."

"They will. Now all we need is a witness who can place her with Mr. Hardy the night of his death, and we can have her arrested and charged with murder," he replied.

"Chance would be a fine thing, Mr. Kemp," she said heavily.

"Don't give up hope," he instructed. "She's not going to get away with your inheritance. I promise."

She managed a smile. "Thanks."

But she wasn't really convinced. She went home that afternoon feeling lost and alone. She'd told Curt the good news after Violet had gone home with Kemp. Curt had been as relieved as she had, but there was still the problem of probate. Everything was in Janet's name, as their father had instructed. Janet had the insurance money. Nobody could do anything with the estate until the will was probated and

Janet had to sign the papers for that. It was a financial nightmare.

There was a message on the answering machine when Libby got home. She pushed the Play button and her heart sank right to her ankles.

"This is the loan officer at Jacobsville Savings and Loan," came the pleasant voice. "We just wanted to remind you that your loan payment was due three days ago. Please call us if there's a problem." The caller gave her name and position and her telephone number. The line went dead.

Libby sat down beside the phone and just stared at it. Curt had told her already that they weren't going to be able to make the payment. Jordan had assured her that he wasn't going to loan her the money to pay it. There was nobody else they would feel comfortable asking. She put her face in her hands and let the tears fall. The financial establishment would repossess the ranch. It wouldn't matter where Janet was or what state the probate action was in. They were going to lose their home.

She went out to the barn and ran the curry comb over Bailey, her father's horse. He was the last horse they had.

The barn leaked. It was starting to rain and Libby felt raindrops falling on her shoulder through a rip in the tin roof from a small tornado that had torn through a month earlier. The straw on the floor of the barn needed changing, but the hay crop had drowned in the flooding. They'd have to buy some. Libby looked down at her worn jeans, at the small hand resting on them. The tiger eye ring her father had given her looked ominous in the darkened barn. She sighed and turned back to the horse.

"Bailey, I don't know what we're going to do," she told the old horse, who neighed as if he were answering her.

The sound of a vehicle pulling up in the yard diverted her. She looked down the long aisle of the barn to see Jordan's pickup truck sitting at the entrance. Her heart skipped as he got out and came striding through the dirty straw, his cotton shirt speckled with raindrops that had escaped the wide brim of his white straw hat.

"What do you want?" she asked, trying to ignore him to finish her grooming job on the horse.

"My two new thoroughbreds are missing."

She turned, the curry comb suspended in her small hand. "And you think we took them?" she asked incredulously. "You honestly think we'd steal from you, even if we were starving?"

He averted his face, as if the question had wounded him.

"Please leave," she said through her teeth.

He rammed his hands into his pockets and moved a step closer, looking past her to Bailey. "That horse is useless for ranch work. He's all of twenty."

"He's my horse," she replied. "I'm not getting rid of him, whatever happens."

She felt his lean, powerful body at her back. "Libby," he began. "About that bank loan…"

"Curt and I are managing just fine, thanks," she said without turning.

His big, strong hands came down heavily on her shoulders, making her jump. "The bank president is a good friend of the Merrills."

She pulled away from him and looked up, her unspoken fears in her green eyes. "They can't do anything to us without Janet," she told him. "She has legal power of attorney."

"Damn it, I know that!" he muttered. "But it's not going to stop the bank from foreclosing, don't you see? You can't make the loan payment!"

"What business is that of yours?" she asked bitterly.

He drew in a slow breath. "I can talk to the president of the Jacobsville Merchant Bank for you," he said. "He might be willing to work out something for the land. You and Curt can't work it, anyway, and you don't have the capital to invest in it. The best you could do is sell off your remaining cattle and give it up.''

She couldn't even manage words. She had no options at all and he had to know it. She could almost hate him.

"We can't sell anything," she said harshly. "I told you, Janet has power of attorney. And she was named in Daddy's will as the sole holder of the property. We can't even sell a stick of furniture. We're going to have to watch the bank foreclose, Jordan, because Janet has our hands tied. We're going to lose everything Daddy worked for, all his life…''

Her lower lip trembled. She couldn't even finish the sentence.

Jordan stepped forward and wrapped her up tight in his arms, holding her while she cried. "Damn, what a mess!''

She beat a small fist against his massive chest. "Why?'' she moaned. "Why?''

His arms tightened. "I don't know, baby," he whispered at her ear, his voice deep and soothing. "I wish I did.''

She nuzzled closer, drowning in the pleasure of being close to him. It had been so long since he'd held her.

His chest rose and fell heavily. "Kemp's detective hasn't tracked her down yet?''

"Not yet. But she didn't…kill Daddy. The autopsy showed that he died of a heart attack.''

"That's something, I guess," he murmured.

"But Violet's daddy was poisoned," she added quietly, her eyes open as they stared past Jordan's broad chest toward his truck parked at the front of the barn. "So they'll still get her for murder, if they can ever find her.''

"Poor Violet," he said.

"Yes.''

His hand smoothed her hair. It tangled in the wavy soft strands. "You smell of roses, Libby," he murmured deeply, and the pressure of his arms changed in some subtle way.

She could feel the sudden tautness of his lean body against her, the increasing warmth of his embrace. But he'd taken Julie's side against her and she wasn't comfortable being in his arms anymore.

She tried to pull away, but he wouldn't let her.

"Don't fight me," he said gruffly. "You know you don't want to."

"I don't?"

He lifted his head and looked down into her misty and wet green eyes. His voice was deep with feeling. "You haven't stopped wanting me."

"I want hot chocolate, too, Jordan, but it still gives me migraine, so I don't drink it," she said emphatically.

His dark eyebrows lifted. "That's cute. You think you convinced me?"

"Sure," she lied.

He laughed mirthlessly, letting his dark eyes fall to her lips. "Let's see."

He bent, drawing his lips slowly, tenderly, across her mouth in a teasing impression of a kiss. He was lazy and gentle and after a few seconds of imitating a plank of wood, her traitorous body betrayed her.

She relaxed into the heat of his body with a shaky little sigh and found herself enveloped in his arms. He kissed her again, hungrily this time, without the tenderness of that first brief exchange.

She moaned and tried to protest the sudden crush of his lean hand at the base of her spine, rubbing her body against him. But he didn't give her enough breath or strength to protest and the next thing she knew, she was on her back in a stall of fresh hay and his body was completely covering hers.

"No, Jordan," she protested weakly.

"Yes," he groaned. His long leg slid lazily against hers, and between them, while his big, warm hands smoothed blatantly over her ribcage, his thumbs sliding boldly right over her breasts. "Don't think," he whispered against her parted lips. "Just give in. I won't hurt you."

"I know that," she whispered. "But..."

He nibbled on her lower lip. His thumbs edged out gently and found her nipples. They moved lazily, back and forth, coaxing the tips into hard little nubs. She shivered with unexpected pleasure.

He lifted his head and looked into her eyes while he did it again. If she was used to this sort of love play, it certainly didn't show. She was pliable, yielded, absolutely fascinated with what he was doing to her body. She liked it.

That was all he needed to know. His leg became insistent between hers, coaxing them to move apart, to admit the slow, exquisite imprint of his hips between her long legs. It was like that day in the alley beyond her office, when she hadn't cared if all of Jacobsville walked by while he was pressing her aching body against the brick wall. She was drowning in pleasure.

Surely, she thought blindly, it couldn't be wrong to give in to something so sweet! His hands on her body were producing undreamed of sensations. He was giving her pleasure in hot, sweeping waves. He touched her and she ached for more. He kissed her and she lifted against him to find his mouth and coax it into ardor. One of her legs curled helplessly around his powerful thigh and she moaned when he accepted the silent invitation and moved into near intimacy with her.

He was aroused. He was powerful. She felt the hard thrust of him against her body and she wanted to rip off her clothes and invite his hands, his eyes, his body, into complete surrender with her. She wanted to feel the ecstasy she knew he could give her. He was skilled, masterful. He knew what she needed, what she wanted. He could give her pleasure beyond bearing, she knew it.

His lean hands moved under her blouse, searching for closeness, unfastening buttons, invading lace. She felt his fingers brush tenderly, lovingly, over her bare breasts in an intimacy she'd never shared with anyone.

Her dreams of him had been this explicit, but she'd never thought she would live them in such urgent passion. As he

touched her, she arched to help him, moved to encourage
him. Her mouth opened wide under his. She felt his tongue
suddenly thrust into it with violent need.

She moaned loudly, her fingertips gripping the hard muscle of his upper arms as he thrust her blouse and bra up to
her throat and bent at once to put his mouth on her breasts.

The warm, moist contact was shattering. She stiffened
with the shock of pleasure it produced. He tasted her in a
hot, feverish silence, broken only by his urgent breathing
and the rough sigh of her own voice in his ear.

"Yes," he groaned, opening his mouth. "Yes, Libby.
Here. Right here. You and me. I can give you more pleasure than damned Harley ever dreamed of giving you!"

Harley. Harley. She felt her body growing cold. "Harley?" she whispered.

He lifted his head and looked down at her breasts with
grinding urgency. "He's had you."

"He has not!" she exclaimed, shocked.

He scowled, in limbo, caught between his insane need
to possess her and his jealousy of the other man.

She took advantage of his indecision by jerking out of
his arms and pulling her blouse down as she dragged herself out of the stall. She groped for fastenings while she
flushed with embarrassment at what she'd just let him do
to her.

She looked devastated. Her hair was full of straw, like
her clothes. Her green eyes were wild, her face flushed, her
mouth swollen.

He got to his feet, still in the grip of passion, and started
toward her. His hat was off. His hair was wild, from her
searching fingers, and his shirt was half-open over hair-
matted muscle.

"Come back here," he said huskily, moving forward.

"No!" she said firmly, shivering. "I'm not standing in
for Julie Merrill!"

The words stopped him in his tracks. He hesitated, his
brows meeting over turbulent dark eyes.

"Remember Julie? Your girlfriend?" she persisted shakily. Throwing his lover in his face was a way to cover her hurt for the insinuation he'd made about her and Harley. "What in the world would she think if she could see you now?"

He straightened, but with an effort. His body was raging. He wanted Libby. He'd never wanted anyone, anything, as much as he wanted her.

"Julie has nothing to do with this," he ground out. "I want you!"

"For how long, Jordan?" she asked bitingly. "Ten minutes? Thirty?"

He blinked. His mind wasn't working.

"I am nobody's one-night stand," she flashed at him. "Not even yours!"

He took a deep breath, then another one. He stared at her blankly while he tried to stop thinking about how sweet it was to feel her body under his hands.

"I want you to leave, now," she repeated, folding her arms over her loose bra. She could feel the swollen contours of her breasts and remembered with pure shame how it felt to have him touching and kissing them.

"That isn't what you wanted five minutes ago," he reminded her flatly.

She closed her eyes. "I'm grass-green and stupid," she said curtly. "It wouldn't be the first time an experienced man seduced an innocent girl."

"Don't make stupid jokes," he said icily. "You're no innocent."

"You believe what you like about me, Jordan, it doesn't matter anymore," she interrupted him. "I've got work to do. Why don't you go home?"

He glared at her, frustrated desire riding him hard. He cursed himself for ruining everything by bringing up Harley Fowler. "You're a hard woman, Libby," he said. "Harder than I ever realized."

"Goodbye, Jordan," she said, and she turned away to pick up the curry comb she'd dropped.

He gave her a furious glare and stormed out of the barn to his truck. Bailey jumped as Jordan slammed the door and left skid marks getting out of the driveway. She relaxed then, grateful that she'd managed to save herself from that masterful seduction. She'd had a close call. She had to make sure that Jordan never got so close to her again. She couldn't trust him. Not now.

Chapter Eight

Janet was still in hiding before the primary election and probate hadn't begun. But plenty had changed in Jacobsville. Libby and Curt had been forced to move out of the farmhouse where they'd grown up, because the bank had foreclosed.

They hadn't said a word to Jordan about it. Curt moved into the bunkhouse at the Wright ranch where he worked. Libby moved into a boardinghouse where two other Jacobsville career women lived.

Bailey would have had to be boarded and Libby didn't have the money. But she worked out a deal with a dude ranch nearby. Bailey would be used for trail rides for people who were nervous of horses and Libby would help on the weekends. It wasn't the ideal solution, but it was the only one she had. It was a wrench to give up Bailey, even though it wasn't going to be forever.

Jordan and Julie Merrill were apparently engaged. Or so Julie was saying, and she was wearing a huge diamond on her ring finger. Her father was using every dirty trick in the book to gain his party's candidacy.

Julie Merrill was vehemently outspoken about some un-named dirty tactics being used against her father in the primary election campaign, and she went on television to make accusations against Calhoun Ballenger.

The next morning, Blake Kemp had her served as the defendant in a defamation lawsuit.

"They're not going to win this case," Julie raged at Jordan. "I want you to get me the best attorney in Austin! We're going to put Calhoun Ballenger right in the gutter where he belongs, along with all these jump-up nouveau riche that think they own our county!"

Jordan, who was one of those jump-ups, gave her a curious look. "Excuse me?" he asked coolly.

"Well, I'm not standing by while Ballenger talks my father's constituents into deserting him!"

"You're the one who's been making allegations, Julie," Jordan said quietly. "To anyone who was willing to listen."

She waved that away. "You have to do that to win elections."

"I'm not going to be party to anything dishonest," Jordan said through his teeth.

Julie backed down. She curled against him and sighed. "Okay. I'll tone it down, for your sake. But you aren't going to let Calhoun Ballenger sue me, are you?"

Jordan didn't know what he was going to do. He felt uneasy at Julie's temperament and her tactics. He'd taken her side against Kemp when she told him that one of the boys at her graduation party had put something in the Culbertson girl's drink and she couldn't turn him in. She'd cried about Libby Collins making horrible statements against her. But Libby had never done such a thing before.

He'd liked being Julie's escort, being accepted by the social crowd she ran around with. But it was getting old and he was beginning to believe that Julie was only playing up to him for money to put into her father's campaign.

Libby had tried to warn him and he'd jumped down her throat. He felt guilty about that, too. He felt guilty about a lot of things lately.

"Listen," he said. "I think you need to step back and take a good look at what you're doing. Calhoun Ballenger isn't some minor citizen. He and his brother own a feedlot that's nationally known. Besides that, he has the support of most of the people in Jacobsville with money."

"My father has the support of the social set," she began.

"Yes, but Julie, they're the old elite. The demographics have changed in Jacobs County in the past ten years. Look around you. The Harts are a political family from the roots up. Their brother is the state attorney general and he's already casting a serious eye on what's going on in the Jacobsville city council, about those police officers the mayor's trying to suspend."

"They can't do anything about that," she argued.

"Julie, the Harts are related to Chief Grier," he said shortly.

She hesitated. For the first time, she looked uncertain.

"Not only that, they're related to the governor and the vice president. And while it isn't well-known locally, Grier's people are very wealthy."

She sat down. She ran a hand through her blond hair. "Why didn't you say this before?"

"I tried to," he pointed out. "You refused to listen."

"But Daddy can't possibly lose the election," she said with a child's understanding of things. "He's been state senator from this district for years and years."

"And now the voters are looking for some new blood," he told her. "Not only in local government, but in state and national government. You and your father don't really move with the times, Julie."

"Surely, you don't think Calhoun can beat Daddy?" she asked huskily.

"I think he's going to," he replied honestly, ramming his hands into his pockets. "He's way ahead of your father in the polls. You know that. You and your father have made some bad enemies trying to have those police officers fired. You've gotten on the wrong side of not only Cash Grier, but the Harts as well. There will be repercussions. I've already heard talk of a complete recall of the mayor and the city council.''

''But the mayor is Daddy's nephew. How could they…?''

''Don't you know anything about small towns?'' he ground out. ''Julie, you've spent too much time in Austin with your father and not enough around here where the elections are decided.''

''This is just a hick town,'' she said, surprised. ''Why should I care what goes on here?''

Jordan's face hardened. ''Because Jacobs County is the biggest county in your father's district. He can't get re-elected without it. You've damaged his campaign by the way you've behaved to Libby Collins.''

''That nobody?'' she scoffed.

''Her father is a direct descendant of old John Jacobs,'' he pointed out. ''They may not have money and they may not be socially acceptable to you and your father, but the Collinses are highly respected here. The reason Calhoun's got such support is because you've tried to hurt Libby.''

''But that's absurd!''

''She's a good person,'' he said, averting his eyes as he recalled his unworthy treatment of her—and of Curt—on Julie's behalf. ''She's had some hard knocks recently.''

''So have I,'' Julie said hotly. ''Most notably, having a lawsuit filed against me for defamation of character by that lawyer Kemp!'' She turned to him. ''Are you going to get me a lawyer, or do I have to find my own?''

Jordan was cutting his losses while there was still time. He felt like ten kinds of fool for the way he'd behaved in the past few weeks. ''I think you'd better do that yourself,'' he replied. ''I'm not going against Calhoun Ballenger.''

She scoffed. ''You'll never get that Collins woman to

like you again, no matter what you do,'' she said haughtily.
''Or didn't you know that she and her brother have for-
feited the ranch to the bank?''

He was speechless. ''They've what?''

''Nobody would loan them the money they needed to
save it,'' she said with a cold smile. ''So the bank president
foreclosed. Daddy had a long talk with him.''

He looked furious. His big fists clenched at his hips.
''That was low, Julie.''

''When you want to win, sometimes you have to fight
dirty,'' she said simply. ''You belong to me. I'm not letting
some nobody of a little dirt rancher take you away from
me. We need you.''

''I don't belong to you,'' he returned, scooping up his
hat. ''In fact, I've never felt dirtier than I do right now.''

She gaped at him. ''I beg your pardon! You can't talk
to me like that!''

''I just did.'' He started toward the door.

''You're no loss, Jordan,'' she yelled after him. ''We
needed your money, but I never wanted you! You're one
of those jump-ups with no decent background. I'm sorry I
ever invited you here the first time. I'm ashamed that I told
my friends I liked you!''

''That makes two of us,'' he murmured icily, and he
went out the door without a backward glance.

Kemp was going over some notes with Libby when Jordan Powell walked into the office without bothering to
knock.

''I'd like to talk to Libby for a minute,'' he said sol-
emnly, hat in hand.

Libby stared at him blankly. ''I can't think what you
have to say,'' she replied. ''I'm very busy.''

''She is,'' Kemp replied. ''I'm due in court in thirty minutes.''

''Then I'll come back in thirty minutes,'' Jordan replied.

''Feel free, but I won't be here. I have nothing to say to

you, Jordan," she told him bluntly. "You turned your back
on me when I needed you the most. I don't need you now.
I never will again."

"Listen," he began impatiently.

"No." She turned back to Kemp. "What were you saying, boss?"

Kemp hesitated. He could see the pain in Jordan's face
and he had some idea that Jordan had just found out the
truth about Julie Merrill. He checked his watch. "Listen, I
can read your writing. Just give me the pad and I'll get to
the courthouse. It's okay," he added when she looked as
if he were deserting her to the enemy. "Really."

She bit her lower lip hard. "Okay."

"Thanks," Jordan said stiffly, as Kemp got up from the
desk.

"You owe me one," he replied, as he passed the taciturn
rancher on the way out the door.

Minutes later, Mabel went into Kemp's office to put
some notes on his desk, leaving Jordan and Libby alone.

"I've made some bad mistakes," he began stiffly. He
hated apologies. Usually, he found ways not to make them.
But he'd hurt Libby too badly not to try.

She was staring at her keyboard, trying not to listen.

"You have to understand what it's been like for me,"
he said hesitantly. He sat down in a chair next to her desk,
with his wide-brimmed hat in his hands. "My people were
like yours, poor. My mother had money, but her people
disinherited her when she married my dad. I never had two
nickels to rub together. I was that Powell kid, whose father
worked for wages, whose mother was reduced to working
as a housekeeper." He stared at the floor with his pride
aching. "I wanted to be somebody, Libby. That's all I ever
wanted. Just to have respect from the people who mattered
in this town." He shrugged. "I thought going around with
Julie would give me that."

"I don't suppose you noticed that her father belongs to

a group of respectable people who no longer have any power around here," she said stiffly.

He sighed. "No, I didn't. I had my head turned. She was beautiful and rich and cultured, and she came at me like a hurricane. I was in over my head before I knew it."

Libby, who wasn't beautiful or rich or cultured, felt her heart breaking. She knew all this, but it hurt to hear him admit it. Because it meant that those hungry, sweet kisses she'd shared with him meant nothing at all. He wanted Julie.

"I've broken it off with her," he said bluntly.

Libby didn't say anything.

"Did you hear me?" he asked impatiently.

She looked up at him with disillusioned eyes. "You believed her. She said I was shacking up with Harley Fowler. She said I attacked her in this office and hurt her feelings. You believed all that, even though you knew me. And when she attacked me in Barbara's Café and on the courthouse steps, you didn't say a thing."

He winced.

"Words don't mean anything, Powell," she said bitterly. "You can sit there and apologize and try to smooth over what you did for the rest of your life, but I won't listen. When I needed you, you turned your back on me."

He drew in a long breath. "I guess I did."

"I can understand that you were flattered by her attention," she said. "But Curt and I have lost everything we had. Our father is dead and we don't even have a home anymore."

He moved his hat in his hands. "You could move in with me."

She laughed bitterly. "Thanks."

"No, listen," he said earnestly, leaning forward.

She held up a hand. "Don't. I've had all the hard knocks I can handle. I don't want anything from you, Jordan. Not anything at all."

He wanted to bite something. He felt furious at his own

stupidity, at his blind allegiance to Julie Merrill and her father, at his naivete in letting them use him. He felt even worse about the way he'd turned on Libby. But he was afraid of what he'd felt for her, afraid of her youth, her changeability. Now he only felt like a fool.

"Thanks for the offer and the apology," she added heavily. "Now, if you'll excuse me, I have to get back to work."

She turned on the computer, brought up her work screen and shut Jordan out of her sight and mind.

He got up slowly and moved toward the door. He hesitated at it, glancing back at her. "What about the autopsy?" he asked suddenly.

She swallowed hard. "Daddy died of a heart attack, just like the doctors said," she replied.

He sighed. "And Violet's father?"

"Was poisoned," she replied.

"Riddle had a lucky escape," he commented. "So did you and Curt."

She didn't look at him. "I just hope they can find her, before she kills some other poor old man."

He nodded. After a minute, he gave her one last soulful glance and went out the door.

Life went on as usual. Calhoun's campaign staff cranked up the heat. Libby spent her free time helping to make up flyers and make telephone calls, offering to drive voters to the polls during the primary election if they didn't have a way to get to the polls.

"You know, I really think Calhoun's going to win," Curt told Libby while they were having a quick lunch together on Saturday, after she got off from work.

She smiled. "So do I. He's got all kinds of support."

He picked at his potato chips. "Heard from Jordan?"

She stiffened. "He came by the office to apologize a few days ago."

He drew in a long breath. "Rumor is that Julie Merrill's courting Duke Wright now."

"Good luck to her. He's still in love with his wife. And he's not quite as gullible as Jordan."

"Jordan wasn't so gullible," he defended his former boss. "When a woman that pretty turns up the heat, most normal men will follow her anywhere."

She lifted both eyebrows. "Even you?"

He grinned. "I'm not normal. I'm a cowboy."

She chuckled and sipped her iced tea. "They're still looking for Janet. I've had an idea," she said.

"Shoot."

"What if we advertise our property for sale in all the regional newspapers?"

"Whoa," he said. "We can't sell it. We don't have power of attorney and the will's not even in probate yet."

"She's a suspected murderess," she reminded him. "Felons can't inherit, did you know? If she's tried and convicted, we might be able to get her to return everything she got from Daddy's estate."

He frowned, thinking hard. "Do you remember Dad telling us about a new will he'd made?"

She blinked. "No."

"Maybe you weren't there. It was when he was in the hospital, just before he died. He could hardly talk for the pain and he was gasping for breath. But he said there was a will. He said he put it in his safest place." He frowned heavily. "I never thought about that until just now, but what if he meant a *new* will, Libby?"

"It wouldn't have been legal if it wasn't witnessed," she said sadly. "He might have written something down and she found it and threw it out. I doubt it would stand up in court."

"No. He went to San Antonio without Janet, about two days before he had the heart attack," he persisted.

"Who did he know in San Antonio?" she wondered aloud.

"Why don't you ask Mr. Kemp to see if his private detective could snoop around?" he queried softly.

She pursed her lips. "It would be a long shot. And we couldn't afford to pay him...."

"Dad had a coin collection that was worth half a million dollars, Libby," Curt said. "It's never turned up. I can't find any record that he ever sold it, either."

Her lips fell open. In the agony of the past few months, that had never occurred to her. "I assumed Janet cashed it in...."

"She had the insurance money," he reminded her, "and the property—or so she assumed. But when we were sorting out Dad's personal belongings, that case he kept the coins in was missing. What if—" he added eagerly "—he took it to San Antonio and left it with someone, along with an altered will?"

She was trying to think. It wasn't easy. If they had those coins, if nothing else, they could make the loan payment.

"I can ask Mr. Kemp if he'll look into it," she said. "He can take the money out of my salary."

"I can contribute some of mine," Curt added.

She felt lighter than she had in weeks. "I'll go ask him right now!"

"Finish your sandwich first," he coaxed. "You've lost weight, baby sister."

She grimaced. "I've been depressed since we had to leave home."

"Yeah. Me, too."

She smiled at him. "But things are looking up!"

She found Kemp just about to leave for the day. She stopped him at the door and told him what she and Curt had been discussing.

He closed the door behind them, picked up the phone, and dialed a number. Libby listened while he outlined the case to someone, most likely the private detective he'd hired to look for Janet.

"That's right," he told the man. "One more thing, there's a substantial coin collection missing as well. I'll ask." He put his hand over the receiver and asked Libby for a description of it, which he gave to the man. He added a few more comments and hung up, smiling.

"Considering the age of those coins and their value, it wouldn't be hard to trace them if they'd been sold. Good work, Libby!"

"Thank my brother," she replied, smiling. "He remembered it."

"You would have, too, I expect, in time," he said in a kindly tone. "Want me to have a talk with the bank president?" he added. "I think he might be more amenable to letting you and Curt back on the property with this new angle in mind. It might be to his advantage," he added in a satisfied tone.

"You mean, if we turn out to have that much money of our own, free and clear, it would make him very uncomfortable if we put it in the Jacobsville Municipal Bank and not his?"

"Exactly."

Her eyes blazed. "Which is exactly where we *will* put it, if we get it," she added.

He chuckled. "No need to tell him that just yet."

Her eyebrows lifted. "Mr. Kemp, you have a devious mind."

He smiled. "What else is new?"

Libby was furious at herself for not thinking of her father's impressive coin collection until now. She'd watched those coins come in the mail for years without really noticing them. But now they were important. They meant the difference between losing their home and getting it back again.

She sat on pins and needles over the weekend, until Kemp heard from the private detective the following Monday afternoon.

He buzzed Libby and told her to come into the office.

He was smiling when she got there. "We found them," he said, chuckling when she made a whoop loud enough to bring Mabel down the hall.

"It's okay," Libby told her coworker, "I've just had some good news for a change!"

Mabel grinned and went back to work.

Libby sat down in the chair in front of Kemp's big desk, smiling and leaning forward.

"Your father left the coins with a dealer who locked them in his safe. He was told not to let Janet have them under any circumstances," he added gently. "Besides that, there was a will. He's got that, too. It's not a self-made will, either. It was done by a lawyer in the dealer's office and witnessed by two people who work for him."

Libby's eyes filled with tears. "Daddy knew! He knew she was trying to cut us out of the will!"

"He must have," he conceded. "Apparently she'd made some comments about what she was going to do when he died. And she'd been harassing him about his health, making remarks about his heart being weak, as well." His jaw clenched. "Whatever the cause, he changed the will in your favor—yours and Curt's. This will is going to stand up in a court of law and it changes the entire financial situation. You and Curt can go home and I'll get the will into probate immediately."

"But the insurance…"

He nodded. "She was the beneficiary for *one* of his insurance policies." He smiled at her surprise. "There's another one, a half-a-million dollar policy, that he left with the same dealer who has the will. You and Curt are co-beneficiaries."

"He didn't contact us!" she exclaimed suddenly.

"Yes, and that's the interesting part," he said. "He tried to contact you and Janet told him that you and Curt were out of the country on an extended vacation. She planned to go and talk to him the very day you made the remarks about

Violet's father and having locks put on your bedroom doors. She ran for her life before she had time to try to get to the rest of your inheritance." He chuckled. "Maybe she had some idea of what the seller was guarding and decided that the insurance policy would hold her for a while without risking arrest."

"Oh, thank God," she whispered, shivering with delight. "Thank God! We can go home!"

"Apparently," he agreed, smiling. "I'm going to drive up to San Antonio today and get those documents and the coin collection."

She was suddenly concerned. "But what if Janet hears about it? She had that friend in San Antonio who called and tried to get us off the property..." She stopped abruptly. "That's why they were trying to get us out of the house! They knew about the coin collection!" She sat back heavily. "But they could be dangerous...."

"Cash Grier is going with me."

She pursed her lips amusedly. "Okay."

He chuckled. "Nobody is going to try to attack me with Grier in the car. Even if he isn't armed."

"Good point," she agreed.

"So call your brother and tell him the news," he said. "And stop worrying. You're going to land on your feet, Libby."

"How's Violet?" she asked without thinking.

He stood up, his hands deep in his pockets. "She and her mother are distraught, as you might imagine. They never realized that Mr. Hardy had been the victim of foul play. I've tried to keep it out of the papers, but when Janet's caught, it's going to be difficult."

"Is there anything I can do?"

He smiled. "Take them a pizza and let Violet talk to you about it," he suggested. "She misses working here."

"I miss her, too."

He shifted, averting his gaze. "I offered to let her come back to work here."

"You did?" she asked, enthused.

"She's going to think about it," he added. "You might, uh, tell her how short-handed we are here, and that the temporary woman we got had to quit. Maybe she'll feel sorry for us and come back."

She smiled. "I'll do my best."

He looked odd. "Thanks," he said stiffly.

Chapter Nine

The very next day, Kemp came into the office grinning like a lottery winner. He was carrying a cardboard box, in which was a mahogany box full of rare gold coins, an insurance policy, a few personal items that had belonged to Riddle Collins and a fully executed new will.

Libby had to sit down when Kemp presented her with the hard evidence of her father's love for herself and Curt.

"The will is legal," he told her. "I'm going to take it right to the courthouse and file it. It will supercede the will that Janet probably still has in her possession. You should take the coins to the bank and put them in a safe-deposit box until you're ready to dispose of them. The dealer said he'll buy them from you at market value any time you're ready to sell them."

"But I'll have to use them as collateral for a loan to make the loan payment…"

"Actually, no, you won't," Kemp said with a smile, drawing two green-covered passbooks out of the box and handing them to her.

"What are these?" she asked blankly.

"Your father had two other bank accounts, both in San Antonio." He smiled warmly. "There's more than enough there to pay off the mortgage completely so that the ranch is free and clear. You'll still have a small fortune left over. You and your brother are going to be rich, Libby. Congratulations."

She cried a little, both for her father's loving care of them even after death and for having come so close to losing everything.

She pulled a tissue out of the pocket of her slacks and wiped her red eyes. "I'll take these to the Jacobsville Municipal Bank right now," she said firmly, "and have the money transferred here from San Antonio. Then I'll have them issue a cashier's check to pay off the other bank," she added with glee.

"Good girl. You can phone the insurance company about the death benefit, too. How does it feel, not to have to worry about money?"

She chuckled. "Very good." She eyed him curiously. "Does this mean you're firing me?"

"Well, Libby, you won't really need to work for a living anymore," he began slowly.

"But I love my job!" she exclaimed, and had the pleasure of watching his high cheekbones go ruddy. "Can't I stay?"

He drew in a long breath. "I'd be delighted if you would," he confessed. "I can't seem to keep a paralegal these days."

She smiled, remembering that Callie Kirby had been one, until she'd married Micah Steele. There had been two others after her, but neither had stayed long.

"Then it's settled. I have to go and call Curt!"

"Go to the bank first, Libby," he instructed with a grin.

"And I'll get to the courthouse. Mabel, we're going to be out of the office for thirty minutes!"

"Okay, boss!"

They went down the hall together and they stopped dead.

Violet was back at her desk, across from a grinning Mabel, looking radiant. "You said I could come back," she told Kemp at once, looking pretty and uncertain at the same time.

He drew in a sharp breath and his eyes lingered on her. "I certainly did," he agreed. "Are you staying?"

She nodded.

"How about making a fresh pot of coffee?" he asked.

"Regular?" she asked.

He averted his gaze to the door. "Half and half," he murmured. "Caffeine isn't good for me."

He went out the door, leaving Violet's jaw dropped.

"I told you he missed you," Libby whispered as she followed Kemp out the door and onto the sidewalk.

Libby and Curt were able to go home the next morning. But their arrival was bittersweet. The house had been ransacked in their absence.

"We'd better call the sheriff's office," Curt said angrily, when they'd ascertained that the disorder was thorough. "We'll need to have a report filed on this for insurance purposes."

"Do we even have insurance?"

He nodded. "Dad had a homeowner's policy. I've been keeping up the payments, remember?"

She righted a chair that had been turned over next to the desk her father had used in his study. The filling cabinet had been emptied onto the floor, along with a lot of other documents pertaining to the ranch's business.

"They were looking for that coin collection," Curt

guessed as he picked up the phone. ''I'll bet anything Janet knew about it. She must be running short of cash already!''

''Thank God Mr. Kemp was able to track it down,'' she said.

''Sheriff's department?'' Curt said into the telephone receiver. ''I need you to send someone out to the Collins ranch. That's right, it's just past Jordan Powell's place. We've had a burglary. Yes. Okay. Thanks!'' He hung up. ''I talked to Hayes. He's going to come himself, along with his investigator.''

''I thought he was overseas with his army unit in Iraq,'' she commented.

''He's back.'' He glanced at her amusedly. ''You used to have a case on him, just before you went nuts over Jordan Powell.''

She hated hearing Jordan's name mentioned. ''Hayes is nice.''

''So he is.'' He toyed with the telephone cord. ''Libby, Jordan's having some bad times lately. His association with the Merrills has made him enemies.''

''That was his choice,'' she reminded her brother.

''He was good to us, when Dad died.''

She knew that. It didn't help. Her memories of Jordan's betrayal were too fresh. ''Think I should do anything before they get here?''

''Make coffee,'' he suggested dryly. ''Hayes's investigator is Mack Hughes, and he lives on caffeine.''

''I'll do that.''

Sheriff Hayes Carson pulled up at the front steps in his car, a brightly polished black vehicle with all sorts of antennae sticking out of it. The investigator, Mack Hughes, pulled up beside it in his black SUV with a deck of lights on the roof.

"Thanks for coming so quickly," Curt said, shaking hands with both men. "You remember my sister, Libby."

"Hello, Elizabeth," Hayes said with a grin, having always used her real first name instead of the nickname most people called her by. He was dashing, with blond hair and dark eyes, tall and muscular and big. He was in his mid-thirties; one tough customer, too. He and Cash Grier often went head-to-head in disputes, although they were good colleagues when there was an emergency.

"Hi, Hayes," she replied with a smile. "Hello, Mack."

Mack, tall and dark, nodded politely. "Let's see what you've got."

They ushered the law enforcement officers inside and stood back while they went about searching for clues.

"Any idea who the perpetrators were?" Hayes murmured while Mack looked around.

"Someone connected to our stepmother, most likely," Libby commented. "Dad had a very expensive coin collection and some secret bank accounts that even we didn't know about. If that's what they were looking for, they're out of luck. Mr. Kemp tracked them to San Antonio. Everything's in the bank now and a new will we recovered is in the proper hands."

Hayes whistled softly. "Lucky for you."

There was a sudden commotion in the front yard, made by a truck skidding to a stop between the two law enforcement vehicles. A dusty, tired Jordan Powell came up the steps, taking them two at a time, and stopped abruptly in the living room.

"What's happened?" he asked at once, his eyes homing to Libby with dark concern.

"The house was ransacked," Hayes told him. "Have you seen anything suspicious?"

"No. But I'll ask my men," Jordan assured them. He looked at Libby for a long time. "You okay?"

"Curt and I are fine, thanks," she said in a polite but reserved tone.

Jordan looked around at the jumble of furniture and paper on the floor, along with lamps and broken pieces of ceramic items that had been on the mantel over the fireplace.

"This wasn't necessary," Jordan said grimly. "Even if they were looking for something, they didn't have to break everything in the house."

"It was malicious, all right," Hayes agreed. He moved just in front of Libby. "I heard from Grier that you've had two confrontations with Julie Merrill, one of them physically violent. She's also been implicated in acts of vandalism. I want to know if you think she might have had any part in this."

Libby glanced at Jordan apprehensively.

"It could be a possibility," Jordan said, to her dismay. "She was jealous of Libby and I've just broken with Julie and her father. She didn't take it well."

"I'll add her to the list of suspects," Hayes said quietly. "But I have to tell you, she isn't going to like being accused."

"I don't care," Curt replied, answering for himself as well as Libby. "Nobody has a right to do something like this."

"Boss!" Mack called from the back porch. "Could you ask the Collinses to come out here, please?"

Curt stood aside to let Libby go first. On the small back stoop, Mack was squatting down, looking at a big red gas can. "This yours?" he asked Curt.

Curt frowned. "We don't have one that big," he replied. "Ours is locked up in the outbuilding next to the barn."

Mack and Hayes exchanged curious looks.

"There's an insurance policy on the house," Libby remarked worriedly. "It's got Janet, our stepmother, listed as beneficiary."

"That narrows down the suspects," Hayes remarked.

"Surely she wouldn't…" Libby began.

"You've made a lot of trouble for her," Jordan said grimly. "And now she's missed out on two savings accounts and a will that she didn't even know existed."

"How did you know that?" Libby asked belligerently.

"My cousin owns the Municipal Bank," Jordan said nonchalantly.

"He had no business telling you anything!" Libby protested.

"He didn't, exactly," Jordan confessed. "I heard him talking to one of his clerks about opening the new account for you and setting up a safe-deposit box."

"Eavesdropping should be against the law," she muttered.

"I'll make a note of it," Hayes said with a grin.

She grinned back. "Thanks, Hayes."

He told Mack to start marking evidence to be collected. "We'll see if we can lift any latent prints," he told the small group. "If it was Janet, or someone she hired, they'll probably have been wearing gloves. If it was Julie Merrill, we might get lucky."

"I hope we can connect somebody to it," Libby said wearily, looking around. "If for no other reason than to make them pay to help have this mess cleaned up!"

"I'll take care of that," Jordan said at once, and reached for his cell phone.

"We don't need—!" Libby began hotly.

But Jordan wasn't listening. He was talking to Amie at his ranch, instructing her to phone two housekeepers she knew who helped her with heavy tasks and send them over to the Collins place.

"You might as well give up," Hayes remarked dryly.

"Once Jordan gets the bit between his teeth, it would take a shotgun to stop him. You know that."

She sighed angrily. "Yes. I know."

Hayes pushed his wide-brimmed hat back off his forehead and smiled down at Libby. "Are you doing anything Saturday night?" he asked. "They're having a campaign rally for Calhoun's supporters at Shea's."

"I know, I'm one of them," she replied, smiling. "Are you going to be there?"

He shrugged. "I might as well. Somebody'll have a beer too many and pick a fight, I don't doubt. Tiny the bouncer will have his hands full."

"Great!" she said enthusiastically.

Jordan was eavesdropping and not liking what he heard. He wanted to tell Hayes to back off. He wanted to tell Libby what he felt. But he couldn't get the words out.

"If you two are moving back in," Hayes added, "I think we'd better have somebody around overnight. I've got two volunteer deputies in the Sheriff's Posse who would be willing, I expect, if you'll keep them in coffee."

She smiled. "I'd be delighted. Thanks, Hayes. It would make me feel secure. We've got a shotgun, but I don't even know where it is."

"You could both stay with me until Hayes gets a handle on who did this," Jordan volunteered.

"No, thanks," Libby said quietly, trying not to remember that Jordan had already asked her to do that. No matter how she felt about the big idiot, she wasn't going to step into Julie Merrill's place.

"This is our home," Curt added.

Jordan drew in a long, sad breath. "Okay. But if you need help…"

"We'll call Hayes, thanks," Libby said, turning back to the sheriff. "I need to tidy up the kitchen. Is it all right?"

Hayes went with her into the small room and looked

around. There wasn't much damage in there and nothing was broken. "It looks okay. Go ahead, Libby. I'll see you Saturday, then?"

She grinned up at him. "Of course."

He grinned back and then rejoined the men in the living room. "I'm going to talk to my volunteers," he told Curt. "I'll be in touch."

"Thanks a lot, Hayes," Curt replied.

"Just doing my job. See you, Jordan."

"Yeah." Jordan didn't offer to shake hands. He glared after the other man as he went out the front door.

"I can clean my own house," Libby began impatiently.

Jordan met her eyes evenly. "I've made a lot of mistakes. I've done a lot of damage. I know I can't make it up to you in one fell swoop, but let me do what I can to make amends. Will you?"

Libby looked at her brother, who shrugged and walked away, leaving her to deal with Jordan alone.

"Some help you are," Libby muttered at his retreating back.

"I don't like the idea of that gas can," Jordan said, ignoring her statement. "You can't stay awake twenty-four hours a day. If Janet is really desperate enough to set fire to the house trying to get her hands on the insurance money, neither you nor Curt is going to be safe here."

"Hayes is getting us some protection," she replied coolly.

"I know that. But even deputies have to use the bathroom occasionally," he said flatly. "Why won't you come home with me?"

She lifted her chin. "This is my place, mine and Curt's. We're not running anymore."

He sighed. "I admire your courage, Libby. But it's misplaced this time."

She turned away. "I've got a lot to do, Jordan. Thanks anyway."

He caught her small waist from behind and held her just in front of him. His warm breath stirred the hair at the back of her head. "I was afraid."

"Of...what?" she asked, startled.

His big hands contracted. "You're very young, even for a woman your age," he said stiffly. "Young women are constantly changing."

She turned in his hold, curious. She looked up at him without understanding. "What has that got to do with anything?"

He reached out and traced her mouth with his thumb. He looked unusually solemn. "You really don't know, do you?" he asked quietly. "That's part of the problem."

"You aren't making any sense."

"I am. You're just not hearing what I'm saying." He bent and kissed her softly beside her ear, drawing away almost at once. "Never mind. You'll figure it out one day. Meanwhile, I'm going to do a better job of looking after you."

"I can—"

He interrupted at once. "If you say 'look after myself,' so help me, I'll...!"

She glared at him.

He glared back.

"You're up against someone formidable, whoever it is," he continued. "I'm not letting anything happen to you, Libby."

"Fat lot you cared before," she muttered.

He sighed heavily. "Yes, I know. I'll eat crow without catsup if it will help you trust me again."

"Julie's very pretty," she said reluctantly.

"She isn't a patch on you, butterfly," he said quietly.

She hesitated. But she wasn't giving in easily. He'd hurt

her. No way was she going to run headfirst into his arms the first time he opened them.

She watched him suspiciously.

His broad chest rose and fell. "Okay. We'll do it your way. I'll see you at Shea's."

"You're the enemy," she pointed out. "You're not on Calhoun's team."

He shrugged. "A man can change sides, can't he?" he mused. "Meanwhile, if you need me, I'll be at the house. If you call, I'll come running."

She nodded slowly. "All right."

He smiled at her.

Curt came back in. He was as cool to Jordan as his sister. The older man shrugged and left without another word.

"Now he's changed sides again," Libby told Curt when Jordan was gone.

"Jordan's feeling his age, Libby," Curt told her. "And some comments were made by his cowboys about that kiss they saw."

Her eyebrows arched. "What?"

He sighed. "I never had the heart to tell you. But one of the older hands said Jordan was trying to rob the cradle. It enraged Jordan. But it made him think, too. He knows how sheltered you've been. I think he was trying to protect you."

"From what?"

"Maybe from a relationship he didn't think you were ready for," he replied. "Julie was handy, he'd dated her a time or two, and she swarmed all over him just about the time he was drawing back from you. I expect he was flattered by her attention and being invited into that highbrow social set that shut out his mother after she was disinherited because she married his father. The local society women just turned their backs on her. She was never invited any-

where ever again. Jordan felt it keenly, that some of his
playmates weren't allowed to invite him to their houses.''

"I didn't know it was so hard on him. He's only told
me bits and pieces about his upbringing.''

"He doesn't advertise it," he added. "She gave up everything to marry his father. She worked as a housekeeper
in one of the motels owned by her father's best friend. It
was a rough upbringing for Jordan.''

"I can imagine." She sighed, unable to prevent her heart
from thawing.

Shea's was filled to capacity on Saturday evening. Cash
Grier got a lot of attention because he brought Tippy with
him. She looked good despite her ordeals, except for the
small indications of healing cuts on her lovely face. She
was weak and still not totally recovered and it showed.
Nevertheless, she was still the most beautiful woman in the
room. But she had eyes only for Cash and that showed, too.

When they got on the dance floor together, Libby was
embarrassed to find herself staring wistfully at them. Tippy
melted into Cash's tall body as if she'd found heaven. He
looked that way as well. They clung together to the sound
of an old love song. And when she looked up at him, he
actually stopped dancing and just stared at her.

"They make a nice couple," Jordan said from behind
her.

She glanced up at him. He looked odd. His dark eyes
were quiet, intent on her uplifted face.

"Yes, they do," she replied. "They seem to fit together
very well.''

He nodded. "Dance with me," he said in a deep voice,
and drew her into his arms.

She hesitated, but only for a few seconds. She'd built
dreams on those kisses they'd shared and she thought it
was all over. But the way he was holding her made her

knees weak. His big hand covered hers against his chest and pressed it hard into the warm muscle.

"I've been an idiot," he said at her ear.

"What do you mean?" she wondered aloud, drugged by his closeness.

"I shouldn't have backed off," he replied quietly. "I got cold feet at the very worst time."

"Jordan…"

"…mind if I cut in?" Hayes Carson asked with a grin.

Jordan stopped, his mind still in limbo. "We were talking," he began.

"Plenty of time for that later. Shall we, Libby?" he asked, and moved right in front of Jordan. He danced Libby away before she had a chance to stop him.

"Now that's what I call a jealous man," Hayes murmured dryly, glancing over her shoulder at Jordan. "No need to ask about the lay of the land."

"Jordan doesn't feel that way about me," Libby protested.

"He doesn't?"

She averted her eyes to the crowded dance floor. "He isn't a marrying man."

"Uh-huh."

She glanced up at Hayes, who was still grinning.

She flushed at the look in his eyes.

Across the room, Jordan Powell saw that flush and had to restrain himself from going over there and tearing Libby out of Hayes's embrace.

"What the devil are you doing here?" Calhoun Ballenger asked abruptly.

Jordan glanced at him wryly. "Not much," he murmured. "But I came to ask if you needed another willing ally. I've, uh, changed camps."

Calhoun's eyebrows went up almost to his blond hairline.

"I do like to be on the winning side," Jordan drawled.

Calhoun burst out laughing. "Well, you're not a bad diplomat, I guess," he confessed, holding out his hand. "Welcome aboard."

"My pleasure."

Jordan contrived to drive Libby and Curt home, but he was careful to let Curt go into the ranch house before he cut off the engine and turned to Libby.

"There's been some news," he said carefully.

"About Janet?" she exclaimed.

"About Julie," he corrected. He toyed with a strand of her hair in the dim light of the car interior. "One of Grier's men saw her with a known drug dealer earlier today. She's put her neck in a noose and she doesn't even know it."

"She uses, doesn't she?" she asked.

He shrugged. "Her behavior is erratic. She must."

"I'm sorry. You liked her…"

He bent and kissed her hungrily, pulling her across his lap to wrap her up in his warm, strong arms. "I like you," he whispered against her mouth. "More than I ever dreamed I could!"

She wanted to ask questions, but she couldn't kiss him and breathe at the same time. She gave up and ran her arms up around his neck. She relaxed into his close embrace and kissed him back until her mouth grew sore and swollen.

He sighed into her throat as he held her and rocked her in his arms in the warm darkness.

"Libby, I think we should start going out together."

She blinked. "You and me?"

He nodded. "You and me." He drew back and looked down at her possessively. "I could give up liver and onions, if I had to. But I can't give you up."

"Listen, I don't have affairs…"

He kissed her into silence. "Neither do I. So I guess maybe we won't sleep together after all."

"But if we go out together…" she worried.

He grinned. "You have enough self-restraint for both of us, I'm sure," he drawled. "You can keep me honest."

She drew back a little and noted the position of his big lean hands under her blouse. She looked at him intently.

He cleared his throat and drew his hands out from under the blouse. "Every man is entitled to one little slip. Right?" His eyes were twinkling.

She laughed. "Okay."

He touched her mouth with his one last time. "In that case, you'd better rush inside before I forget to be honest."

"Thanks for bringing us home."

"My pleasure. Lock the doors," he added seriously. "And I'm only a phone call away if you need me. You call me," he emphasized. "Not Hayes Carson. Got that?"

"And since when did I become your personal property?" she asked haughtily.

"Since the minute you let me put my hands under your blouse," he shot right back, laughing. "Think about it."

She got out of the vehicle, dizzy and with her head swimming. In one night, everything had changed.

"Don't worry," he added gently, leaning out the window. "I have enough restraint for both of us!"

Before she could answer him, he gunned the engine and took off down the road.

Chapter Ten

For the next few days, Jordan was at Libby's house more than at his own. He smoothed over hard feelings with her brother and became a household fixture. Libby and Curt filed the insurance claim, paid off the mortgage, and started repurchasing cattle for the small ranch.

Janet was found a couple of days later at a motel just outside San Antonio, with a man. He turned out to be the so-called attorney who'd phoned and tried to get Libby and Curt out of their home. She was arrested and charged with murder in the death of Violet's father. There was DNA evidence taken from the dead man's clothing and the motel room that was directly linked to Janet. It placed her at the motel the night Mr. Hardy died. When she realized the trouble she was in, she tried to make a deal for a reduced sentence. She agreed to confess to the murder in return for a life sentence without hope of parole. But she denied having a gas can. She swore that she never had plans to burn down Riddle Collins's house with his children in it. Nobody paid her much attention. She'd told so many lies.

It was a different story for Julie Merrill. She continued

to make trouble, and not only for Calhoun Ballenger. She was determined that Jordan wasn't going to desert her for little Libby Collins. She had a plan. Two days before the hearing to decide the fate of the police officers who'd arrested her father— Saturday, she put it into practice.

She phoned Libby at work and apologized profusely for all the trouble she'd caused.

"I never meant to be such a pain in the neck," she assured Libby. "I want to make it up to you. You get off at one on Saturdays, don't you? Suppose you come over here for lunch?"

"To your house?" Libby replied warily.

"Yes. I've had our cook make something special," she purred. "And I can tell you my side of the story. Will you?"

Dubious, Libby hesitated.

"Surely you aren't afraid of me?" Julie drawled. "I mean, what could I do to you, even if I had something terrible in mind?"

"You don't need to feed me," Libby replied cautiously. "I don't hold grudges."

"You'll come, then," Julie persisted. "Today at one. Will you?"

It was against her better judgment. But it wasn't a bad idea to keep a feud going, especially now that Jordan seemed really interested in her.

"Okay," Libby said finally. "I'll be there at one."

"Thanks!" Julie said huskily. "You don't know how much I appreciate it! Uh, I don't guess you'd like to bring your brother, too?" she added suddenly.

Libby frowned. "Curt's driving a cattle truck for Duke Wright up to San Antonio today."

"Well, then, another time, perhaps! I'll see you at one." Julie hung up, with a bright and happy note in her voice.

Libby frowned. Was she stupid to go to the woman's home? But why would Julie risk harming her now, with the primary election so close? It was the following Tuesday.

She phoned Jordan. "Guess what just happened?" she asked.

"You've realized how irresistible I am and you're rushing over to seduce me?" he teased. "Shall I turn down the covers on my bed?"

"Stop that," she muttered. "I'm serious."

"So am I!"

"Jordan," she laughed. "Julie just called to apologize. She invited me to lunch."

"Did she?" he asked. "Are you going?"

"I thought I might." She hesitated. "Don't you think it's a good idea, to mend fences, I mean?"

"I don't know, Libby," he replied seriously. "She's been erratic and out of control lately. I don't think it's a good idea. I'd rather you didn't."

"Are you afraid she might tell me something about you that I don't know?" she returned, suspicious.

He sighed. "No. It's not that. She wasn't happy when I broke off with her. I don't trust her."

"What can she do to me in broad daylight?" she laughed. "Shoot me?"

"Of course not," he scoffed.

"Then stop worrying. She only wants to apologize."

"You be careful," he returned. "And phone me when you get home. Okay?"

"Okay."

"How about a movie tonight?" he added. "There's a new mystery at the theater. You can even have popcorn."

"That sounds nice," she said, feeling warm and secure.

"I'll pick you up about six."

"I'll be ready. See you then."

She hung up and pondered over his misgivings. Surely he was overreacting. He was probably afraid Julie might make up a convincing lie about how intimate they'd been. Or perhaps she might be telling the truth. She only knew that she had to find out why Julie wanted to see her in person. She was going.

But something niggled at the back of her mind when she drove toward Julie's palatial home on the Jacobs River. Julie might have wanted to invite Libby over to apologize, but why would she want Curt to come, too? She didn't even know Curt.

Libby's foot lifted off the accelerator. Her home was next door to Jordan's. Julie was furious that Jordan had broken off with her. If the house was gone, Libby and Curt would have to move away again, as they had before…!

Libby turned the truck around in the middle of the road and sped toward her house. She wished she had a cell phone. There was no way to call for help. But she was absolutely certain what was about to happen. And she knew immediately that her stepmother hadn't been responsible for that gas can on the porch.

The question was, who had Julie convinced to set that fire for her? Or would she be crazy enough to try and do it herself?

Libby sped faster down the road. If only there had been state police, a sheriff's deputy, a policeman watching. She was speeding. It was the only time in her life she'd ever wanted to be caught!

But there were no flashing lights, no sirens. She was going to have to try and stop the perpetrator all by herself. She wasn't a big woman. She had no illusions about being able to tackle a grown man. She didn't even have a weapon. Wait. There was a tire tool in the boot! At least, she could threaten with it.

She turned into the road that led to the house. There was no smoke visible anywhere and no sign of any traffic. For the first time, she realized that she could be chasing make-believe villains. Why would she think that Julie Merrill would try to burn her house down? Maybe the strain of the past weeks was making her hysterical after all.

She pulled up in front of the house and got out, grabbing the tire tool out of the back. It wouldn't hurt to look around, now that she was here.

She moved around the side of the house, her heart beating wildly. Her palms were so sweaty that she had to get a better grip on the tire tool. She walked past the chimney, to the corner, and peered around. Her heart stopped.

There was a man there. A young, dark man. He had a can of gasoline. He was muttering to himself as he sloshed it on the back porch and the steps.

Libby closed her eyes and prayed for strength. There was nobody to help her. She had to do this alone.

She walked around the corner with the tire tool raised. "That's enough, you varmint! You're trespassing on private property and you're going to jail. The police are right behind me!"

Startled, the man dropped the gas can and stared wild-eyed at Libby.

Sensing an advantage, she started to run toward him, yelling at the top of her lungs.

To her amazement, he started running down a path behind the house, with Libby right on his heels, still yelling.

Then something happened that was utterly in the realm of fantasy. She heard an engine behind her. An accomplice, she wondered, almost panicking.

Jordan Powell pulled up right beside her in his truck and threw open the passenger door. "Get in!" he called.

She didn't need prompting. She jumped right in beside him, tire tool and all, and slammed the door. "He was dousing the back porch with gas!" she panted. "Don't let him get away!"

"I don't intend to." His face was grim as he stood down

on the accelerator and the truck shot forward on the pasture road, which was no more than tracks through tall grass.

The attempted arsonist was tiring. He was pretty thick in the middle and had short legs. He was almost to a beat-up old car sitting out of sight of the house near the barn when Jordan came alongside him on the driver's side.

"Hold it in the ruts!" he called to Libby.

Just as she grabbed the wheel, he threw open the door and leaped out on the startled, breathless young man, pinning him to the ground.

By the time Libby had the truck stopped, Jordan had the man by his shirt collar and was holding him there.

"Pick up the phone and call Hayes," he called to Libby.

Her hands were shaking, but she managed to dial 911 and give the dispatcher an abbreviated account of what had just happened. She was told that they contacted a deputy who was barely a mile away and he was starting toward the Collins place at that moment.

Libby thanked her nicely and cut off the phone.

"Who put you up to this?" Jordan demanded of the man. "Tell me, or so help me, I'll make sure you don't get out of prison until you're an old man!"

"It was Miss Julie," the young man sobbed. "I never done nothing like this in my life. My daddy works for her and he took some things out of her house. She said she'd turn him over to the police if I didn't do this for her."

"She'd have turned him over anyway, you fool," Jordan said coldly. "She was using you. Do you have any idea what the penalty is for arson?"

He was still sobbing. "I was scared, Mr. Powell."

Jordan relented, but only a little. He looked up as the sound of a siren was heard coming closer.

Libby opened the door of the truck and got out, just as a sheriff's car came flying down the track and stopped just behind the truck.

The deputy was Sammy Tibbs. They both knew him. He'd been in Libby's class in high school.

"What have you got, Jordan?" Sammy asked.

"A would-be arsonist," Jordan told him. "He'll confess if you ask him."

"I caught him pouring gas on my back porch and I chased him with my tire tool. I almost had him when Jordan came along," Libby said with a shy grin.

"Whew," Sammy whistled. "I hope I don't ever run afoul of you," he told her.

"That makes two of us," Jordan said, with a gentle smile for her.

"I assume you'll be pressing charges?" Sammy asked Libby as he handcuffed the young man, who was still out of breath.

"You can bet real money on it," Libby agreed. "And you'll need to pick up Julie Merrill as well, because this man said she told him to do it."

Sammy's hands froze on the handcuffs. "Julie Merrill? The state senator's daughter?"

"That's exactly who I mean," Libby replied. "She called and invited me over to lunch. Since she doesn't like me, I got suspicious and came home instead, just in time to catch this weasel in the act."

"Is this true?" the deputy asked the man.

"Mirandize him first," Jordan suggested. "Just so there won't be any loopholes."

"Good idea," Sammy agreed, and read the suspect his rights.

"Now, tell him," Libby prodded, glaring at the man who'd been within a hair of burning her house down.

The young man sighed as if the weight of the world was sitting on his shoulders. "Miss Merrill had something on my daddy, who works for her. She said if I'd set a fire on Miss Collins's back steps, she'd forget all about it. She just wanted to scare Miss Collins is all. She didn't tell me to burn the whole place down.''

"Arson is arson," Sammy replied. "Don't touch anything," he told Libby. "I'll send our investigator back out there and call the state fire marshal. Arson is hard to prove, but this one's going to be a walk in the park.''

"Thanks, Sammy," Libby said.

He grinned. "What for? You caught him!''

He put the scared suspect in the back of his car and sped off with a wave of his hand.

"That was too damned close," Jordan said, looking down at Libby with tormented eyes. "I couldn't believe it when I saw you chasing him through the field with a tire iron! What if he'd been armed?''

"He wasn't," she said. "Besides, he ran the minute I chased him, just like a black snake.''

He pulled her into his arms and wrapped her up tight. There was a faint tremor in those strong arms.

"You brave idiot," he murmured into her neck. "Thank God he didn't get the fire started first. I can see you running inside to grab all the sentimental items and save them. You'd have been burned alive.''

She grimaced, because he was absolutely right. She'd have tried to save her mementos of her father and mother, at any cost.

"Libby, I think we'd better get engaged," he said suddenly.

She was hallucinating. She said so.

He pulled back from her, his eyes solemn. "You're not hallucinating. If Julie realizes how serious this is between us, she'll back off.''

"She's going to be in jail shortly, she'll have to," she pointed out.

"They can afford bail until her hearing, even so," he replied. "She'll be out for blood. But if she hears about the engagement, it might be enough to make her think twice.''

"I'm not afraid of her," she said, although she really was.

"Humor me," he coaxed, bending to kiss her gently.

She smiled under the warm, comforting feel of his hard mouth on her lips. "Well…"

He nibbled her upper lip. "I'll get you a ring," he whispered.

"What sort?"

"What do you want?"

"I like emeralds," she whispered, standing on tiptoe to coax his mouth down again.

"An emerald, then."

"Nobody would know?"

He chuckled as he kissed her. "We might have to tell a few hundred people, just to make it believable. And we might actually have to get married, but that's okay, isn't it?"

She blinked. "Get…married?"

"That's what the ring's for, Libby," he said against her warm mouth. "Advance notice."

"But…you've always said you never wanted to get married."

"I always said there's the one woman a man can't walk away from," he added. He lifted his head and looked down at her, all the teasing gone. "I can't walk away from you. The past few weeks have been pure hell."

Her eyes widened with unexpected delight.

He traced her eyebrows with his forefinger. "I missed you," he whispered. "It was like being cut apart."

"You wanted Julie," she accused.

He grimaced. "I wanted you to think about what was happening. You've been sheltered your whole life. Duke Wright's wife was just like you. Then she married and had a child and got career-minded. That poor devil lives in hell because she didn't know what she wanted until it was too late!"

She searched his face quietly. "You think I'd want a career."

"I don't know, Libby," he bit off. He looked anguished. "I'm an all-or-nothing kind of man. I can't just stick my toe in to test the water. I jump in headfirst."

He…loved her. She was stunned. She couldn't believe she hadn't noticed, in all this time. Curt had seen it long before this. He'd tried to tell her. But she hadn't believed that a man like Jordan could be serious about someone like her.

Her lips fell apart with a husky sigh. She was on fire. She'd never dreamed that life could be so sweet. "I don't want a career," she said slowly.

"What if you do, someday?" he persisted.

She reached up and traced his firm, jutting chin with her fingertips. "I'm twenty-four years old, Jordan," she said. "If I don't know my own mind by now, I never will."

He still looked undecided.

She put both hands flat on his shirt. Under it, she could feel the muted thunder of his heartbeat. "Why don't we go to a movie?" she asked.

He seemed to relax. He smiled. "We could grab a hamburger for lunch and talk about it," he prompted.

"Okay."

"Then we'll go by the sheriff's department and you can write out a statement," he added.

She grimaced. "I guess I'll have to."

He nodded. "So will I." His eyes narrowed. "I wish I could see the look on Julie's face when the deputy sheriff pulls up in her driveway."

"I imagine she'll be surprised," Libby replied.

Surprised was an understatement. Julie Merrill gaped at the young man in the deputy sheriff's uniform.

"You're joking," she said haughtily. "I…I had nothing to do with any attempted arson!"

"We have a man in custody who'll swear to it," he replied. "You can come peacefully or you can go out the door in handcuffs," he added, still pleasant and respectful. "Your choice, Miss Merrill."

She let out a harsh breath. "This is outrageous!"

"What's going on out here?" Her father, the state senator, came into the hall, weaving a little, and blinked when he saw the deputy. "What's he doing here?" he murmured.

"Your daughter is under arrest, senator," he was told as the deputy suddenly turned Julie around and cuffed her with professional dexterity. "For conspiracy to commit arson."

"Arson?" The senator blinked. "Julie?"

"She sent a man to burn down the Collins place," he was told. "We have two eyewitnesses as well."

The senator gaped at his daughter. "I told you to leave that woman alone," he said, shaking his finger at her. "I told you Jordan would get involved if you didn't! You've cost me the election! Everybody around here will go to the polls Tuesday and vote for Calhoun Ballenger! You've ruined me!"

"Oh, no, sir, she hasn't," the deputy assured him with a grin. "Your nephew, the mayor, did that, by persecuting two police officers who were just doing their jobs." The smile faded. "You're going to see Monday night just how much hot water you've jumped into. That disciplinary hearing is going to be remembered for the next century in Jacobsville."

"Where are you taking my daughter?" the senator snorted.

"To jail, to be booked. You can call your attorney and arrange for a bail hearing whenever you like," the deputy added, with a speaking glance at the older man's condition. "If you're able."

"I'll call my own attorney," Julie said hotly. "Then I'll sue you for false arrest!"

"You're welcome to try," the deputy said. "Come along, Miss Merrill."

"Daddy, do try to sober up!" Julie said scathingly.

"What would be the point?" the senator replied. "Life was so good when I didn't know all about you, Julie. When I thought you were a sweet, kind, innocent woman like your mother…" He closed his eyes. "You killed that girl!"

"I did not! Think what you're saying!" Julie yelled at him.

Tears poured down his cheeks. "She died in my arms…"

"Let's go," the deputy said, tugging Julie Merrill out the door. He closed it on the sobbing politician.

Julie Merrill was lodged in the county jail until her bail hearing the following Monday morning. Meanwhile, Jordan and Libby had given their statements and the would-be arsonist was singing like a canary bird.

The disciplinary hearing for Chief Grier's two police officers was Monday night at the city council meeting.

It didn't take long. Within thirty minutes, the Council had finished its usual business, Grier's officers were cleared of any misconduct, and the surprise guests at the hearing had Jacobsville buzzing for weeks afterward.

Chapter Eleven

Jordan drove Libby to his house in a warm silence. He led her into the big, elegant living room and closed the door behind them.

"Want something to drink?" he asked, moving to a pitcher of iced tea that Amie had apparently left for them, along with a plate of homemade cake, covered with foil. "And a piece of pound cake?"

"I'd love that," she agreed.

He poured tea into two glasses and handed them to her, along with doilies to protect the coffee table from spots. He put cake onto two plates, with forks, and brought them along. But as he bent over the coffee table, he obscured Libby's plate. When he sat down beside her, there was a beautiful emerald solitaire, set in gold, lying on her piece of cake.

"Look at that," he exclaimed with twinkling dark eyes. "Why, it's an engagement ring! I wonder who could have put it there?" he drawled.

She picked it up, breathless. "It's beautiful."

"Isn't it?" he mused. "Why don't you try it on? If it fits," he added slyly, "you might turn into a fairy princess and get your own true prince as a prize!"

She smiled through her breathless delight. "Think so?"

"Darlin', I can almost guarantee it," he replied tenderly. "Want to give it a shot?"

He seemed to hold his breath while he waited for her reply. She had to fight tears. It was the most poignant moment of her entire life.

"Why don't you put it on for me?" she asked finally, watching him lift the ring and slide it onto her ring finger with something like relief.

"How about that?" he murmured dryly. "It's a perfect fit. Almost as if it were made just for you," he added.

She looked up at him and all the humor went out of his face. He held her small hand in his big one and searched her eyes.

"You love emeralds. I bought this months ago and stuck it in a drawer while I tried to decide whether or not it would be suicide to propose to you. Duke Wright's situation made me uncertain. I was afraid you hadn't seen enough of the world, or life, to be able to settle down here in Jacobsville. I was afraid to take a chance."

She moved a step closer. "But you finally did."

He cupped her face in his big, warm hands. "Yes. When I realized that I was spending time with Julie just to keep you at bay. If she'd been a better sort of person, it would have been a low thing to do. I was flattered at her interest and the company I got to keep. But I felt like a traitor when she started insulting you in public. I was too wrapped up in my own uncertainties to do what I should have done."

"Which was what?" she asked softly.

He bent to her soft mouth. "I should have realized that if you really love someone, everything works out." He kissed her tenderly. "I should have told you how I felt and given you a chance to spread your wings if you wanted to. I could have waited while you decided what sort of future you wanted."

She still couldn't believe that he didn't know how she felt. "I was crazy about you," she whispered huskily. "Everybody knew it except you." She reached up and linked her arms around his neck. "Duke's wife wasn't like me, Jordan," she added, searching his dark eyes. "She lived with a domineering father and a deeply religious mother. They taught her that a woman's role in life was to marry and obey her husband. She'd always done what they told her to do. But after she married Duke, she ran wild, probably giving vent to all those feelings of suffocated restriction she'd endured all her life. Getting pregnant on her wedding night was a big mistake for both of them, because then she really felt trapped." She took a deep breath. "If Duke hadn't rushed her into it, she'd have gone off and found her career and come back to him when she knew what she really wanted. It was a tragedy in the making from the very beginning."

"She didn't love him enough," he murmured.

"He didn't love her enough," she countered. "He got her pregnant, thinking it would hold her."

He sighed. "I want children," he said softly. "But not right away. We need time to get to know each other before we start a family, don't we?"

She smiled. "See? You ask me about things. You don't order me around. Duke was exactly the opposite." She traced his mouth with her fingertips. "That's why I stopped going out with him. He never asked me what I wanted to do, even what I wanted to eat when we went out together. He actually ordered meals for me before I could say what

I liked." She glowered. "He ordered me liver and onions and I never went out with him again."

He lifted an eyebrow and grinned. "Darlin', I swear on my horse that I will *never* order you liver and onions." He crossed his heart.

He was so handsome when he grinned like that. Her heart expanded like a balloon with pure happiness. "Actually," she whispered, lifting up to him. "I'd even eat liver and onions for you."

"The real test of love," he agreed, gathering her up hungrily. "And I'd eat squash for you," he offered.

She smiled under the slow, sweet pressure of his mouth. Amie said he'd actually dumped a squash casserole in the middle of the living room carpet to make the point that he never wanted it again.

"This is nice," he murmured, lifting her completely off the floor. "But I can do better."

"Can you really?" she whispered, biting softly at his full lower lip. "Show me!"

He laughed, even though his body was making emphatic statements about how little time there was left for teasing. He was burning.

He put her down on the sofa and crushed her into it with the warm, hard length of his body.

"Jordan," she whispered breathlessly when he eased between her long legs.

"Don't panic," he said against her lips. "Amie's a scream away. Lift up."

She did, and he unfastened the bra and pushed it out of the way under her blouse. He deepened the kiss slowly, seductively, while his lean hands discovered the soft warmth of her bare breasts in a heated silence.

Her head began to spin. He was going to be her husband. She could lie in his arms all night long. They could have children together. After the tragedy of the past few months, it was like a trip to paradise.

She moaned and wrapped her long legs around his hips, urging him even closer. She felt the power and heat of him intimately. Her mouth opened, inviting the quick, hard thrust of his tongue.

"Oh, yes," she groaned into his hard mouth. Her hips lifted into his rhythmically, her breath gasping out at his ear as she clung to him. "Yes. That feels...good!"

A tortured sound worked out of his throat as he pressed her down hard into the soft cushions of the sofa, his hands already reaching for the zipper in the front of her slacks, so far gone that he was mindless.

The sound of footsteps outside the door finally penetrated the fog of passion that lay between them. Jordan lifted his head. Libby looked up at him, dazed and only half aware of the sound.

"Amie," Jordan groaned, taking a steadying breath. "We have to stop."

"Tell her to go away," she whispered, laughing breathlessly.

"You tell her," he teased as he got to his feet. "She gets even in the kitchen. She can make squash look just like a corn casserole."

"Amie's Revenge?"

He nodded. "Amie's Revenge." Jordan paused. "I want to marry you," he said quietly. "I want it with all my heart."

She had to fight down tears to answer him. "I want it, too."

He drew her close, over his lap, and when he kissed her, it was with such breathless tenderness that she felt tears threatening again.

She slid her arms around his neck and kissed him back with fervent ardor. But he put her gently away.

"You don't want to ravish me?" she exclaimed. "You said once that you could do me justice in thirty minutes!"

"I lied," he said, chuckling. "I'd need two hours. And Amie's skulking out in the hall, waiting for an opportunity to congratulate us," he added in a whisper. "We can't possibly shock her so soon before the wedding."

She hesitated. "So soon…?"

"I want to get married as quickly as possible," he informed her. "All we need is the blood tests, a license, and I've already got us a minister. Unless you want a formal wedding in a big church with hundreds of guests," he added worriedly.

"No need, since you've already got us a minister," she teased.

He relaxed. "Thank God! The idea of a morning coat and hundreds of people…"

She was kissing him, so he stopped talking.

Just as things were getting interesting, there was an impatient knock at the door. "Well?" Amie called through it.

"She said yes!" Jordan called back.

The door opened and Amie rushed in, grinning from ear to ear.

"She hates squash," he said in a mock whisper.

"I won't ever make it again," Amie promised.

He hugged her. After a minute, Libby joined them. She hugged the housekeeper, too.

"Welcome to the family!" Amie laughed.

And that was the end of any heated interludes for the rest of the evening.

The next few days went by in a blur of activity. When the votes were counted on Tuesday at the primary election,

Senator Merrill lost the Democratic candidacy by a ten-to-one margin. A recall of the city fathers was announced, along with news of a special election to follow. Councilman Culver and the mayor were both implicated in drug trafficking, along with Julie Merrill. Julie had managed to get bail the day before the primary, but she hadn't been seen since. She was also still in trouble for the arson conspiracy. Her father had given an impressive concession speech, in front of the news media, and congratulated Calhoun Ballenger with sincerity. It began to be noticed that he improved when his daughter's sins came to light. Apparently he'd been duty-bound to try and protect her, and it had almost killed his conscience. He'd started drinking heavily, and then realized that he was likely to lose his state senate seat for it. He'd panicked, gone to the mayor, and tried to get the charges dropped.

One irresponsible act had cost Senator Merrill everything. But, he told Calhoun, he still had his house and his health. He'd stand by his daughter, of course, and do what he could for her. Perhaps retirement wouldn't be such a bad thing. His daughter could not be reached for comment. She was now being hunted by every law enforcement officer in Texas and government agents on the drug charges, which were formidable. Other unsavory facts were still coming to light about her doings.

Jordan finally understood why Libby had tried so hard to keep him out of Julie's company and he apologized profusely for refusing to listen to her. Duke Wright's plight had made him somber and afraid, especially when he realized how much he loved Libby. He was afraid to take a chance on her. He had plenty of regrets.

Libby accepted his apology and threw herself into politics as one of Calhoun's speechwriters, a job she loved. But, she told Jordan, she had no desire to do it for a pro-

fession. She was quite happy to work for Mr. Kemp and
raise a family in Jacobsville.

On the morning of Libby's marriage to Jordan, she was
almost floating with delight. "I can't believe the things that
have happened in two weeks," Libby told her brother at
the church door as they waited for the music to go down
the aisle together. "It's just amazing!"

"For a small town, it certainly is," he agreed. He
grinned. "Happy?"

"Too happy," she confessed, blushing. "I never dreamed
I'd be marrying Jordan."

"I did. He's been crazy about you for years, but Duke
Wright's bad luck really got to him. Fortunately, he did see
the light in time."

She took a deep breath as the first strains of the wedding
march were heard. "I'm glad it's just us and not a crowd,"
she murmured.

He didn't speak. His eyes twinkled as he opened the
door.

Inside, all the prominent citizens of Jacobsville were sitting in their pews, waiting for the bride to be given away
by her brother. Cash Grier was there with Tippy. So were
Calhoun Ballenger and Abby, Justin Ballenger and Shelby
Jacobs Ballenger. And the Hart brothers, all five of them
including the attorney general, with their wives. The Tremaynes. Mr. Kemp, with Violet! The Drs. Coltrain and Dr.
Morris and Dr. Steele and their wives. Eb Scott and his
wife. Cy Parks and his wife. It was a veritable who's who
of the city.

"Surprise," Curt whispered in her ear, and tugged her
along down the aisle. She was adorned in a simple white
satin gown with colorful embroidery on the bodice and
puffy sleeves, a delicate veil covering her face and shoul-

ders. She carried a bouquet of lily of the valley and pink roses.

Jordan Powell, in a soft gray morning coat and all the trappings, was waiting for her at the altar with the minister. He looked handsome and welcoming and he was smiling from ear to ear.

Libby thought back over the past few agonizing weeks and realized all the hardships and heartache she'd endured made her truly appreciate all the sweet blessings that had come into her life. She smiled through her tears and stopped at Jordan's side, her small hand searching blindly for his as she waited to speak her vows. She'd never felt more loved or happier than she was at that moment. She only wished her parents had lived to see her married.

Just after the wedding, there was a reception at the church fellowship hall, catered by Barbara's Café. The wedding cake was beautiful, with a colorful motif that exactly matched the embroidery on Libby's wedding gown.

She and Jordan were photographed together cutting the cake and then interacting with all their unexpected guests. The only sticky moment was when handsome Hayes Carson bent to kiss Libby.

"Careful, Hayes," Jordan said from right beside him. "I'm watching you!"

"Great idea," Hayes replied imperturbably and grinned. "You could use a few lessons."

And he kissed Libby enthusiastically while Jordan fumed.

When they were finally alone, hours later in Galveston, Jordan was still fuming about that kiss.

"You know Hayes was teasing," she said, coaxing him into her arms. "But I'm not. I've waited twenty-four years for this,'' she added with a wry smile. "I have great expectations.''

He drew her close with a worldly look. "And I expect to satisfy them fully!''

"I'm not going to be very good at this, at first," she said breathlessly, when he began to undress her. "Is it all right?''

He smiled tenderly. "You're going to be great at it," he countered. "The only real requirement is love. We're rich in that.''

She relaxed a little, watching his dark eyes glow as he uncovered the soft, petal-pink smoothness of her bare skin. She was a little nervous. Nobody had seen her undressed since she was a little girl.

Jordan realized that and it made him even more gentle. He'd never been with an innocent, but he knew enough about women that it wasn't going to be a problem. She loved him. He wanted nothing more than to please her.

When she was standing in just her briefs, he bent and smoothed his warm mouth over the curve of her breasts. She smelled of roses. There was a faint moisture under his lips, which he rightly attributed to fear.

He lifted his head and looked down into her wide, uncertain eyes. "Women have been doing this since the dawn of time," he whispered. "If it wasn't fun, nobody would want to do it. Right?''

She laughed nervously. "Right.''

He smiled tenderly. "So just relax and let me drive. It's going to be a journey you'll never forget.''

Her hands went to his tie. "Okay. But I get to make suggestions,'' she told him impishly, and worked to unfasten the tie and then his white shirt. She opened it over a bronzed chest thick with dark, soft hair. He felt furry. But

under the hair was hard, warm muscle. She liked the way
he felt.

He kissed her softly while he coaxed her hands to his
belt. She hesitated.

"Don't agonize over it," he teased, moving her hands
aside to unfasten it himself. "We'll go slow."

"I'm not really a coward," she whispered unsteadily.
"It's just uncharted territory. I've never even looked at pictures…"

He could imagine what sort of pictures she was talking
about. He only smiled. "Next time, you'll be a veteran and
it won't intimidate you."

"Are you sure?" she asked.

He bent to her mouth again. "I'm sure."

His warm lips moved down her throat to her breasts, but
this time they weren't gently teasing. They were invasive
and insistent as they opened on the hard little nubs his
caresses had already produced. When his hands moved her
hips lazily against the hard thrust of his powerful body, she
began to feel drugged.

She'd thought it would be embarrassing and uncomfortable to make love in the light. But Jordan was slow and
thorough, easing her into an intimacy beyond anything
she'd ever dreamed. He cradled her against him on the big
bed, arousing her to such a fever pitch that when he removed the last bit of her clothing, it was a relief to feel the
coolness of the room against her hot skin. And by the time
he removed his own clothes, she was too hungry to be
embarrassed. In fact, she was as aggressive as he was,
starving for him in the tempestuous minutes that followed.

She remembered the first kiss they'd shared, beside her
pickup truck at his fence. She'd known then that she'd do
anything he wanted her to do. But this was far from the
vague dreams of fulfillment she'd had when she was alone.

She hadn't known that passion was like a fever that nothing could quench, that desire brought intense desperation. She hadn't known that lovemaking was blind, deaf, mute slavery to a man's touch.

"I would die for you," Jordan whispered huskily at her ear as he moved slowly into total possession with her trembling body.

"Will it…hurt?" she managed in a stranger's voice as she hesitated just momentarily at the enormity of what was happening to her.

He laughed sensuously as he began to move lazily against her. "Are you kidding?" he murmured. And with a sharp, deft movement, he produced a sensation that lifted her clear of the bed and against him with an unearthly little cry of pleasure.

From there, it was a descent into total madness. She shivered with every powerful thrust of his body. She clung to him with her arms, her legs, her soul. She moaned helplessly as sensation built on sensation, until she was almost screaming from the urgent need for satisfaction.

She heard her own voice pleading with him, but she couldn't understand her own words. She drove for fulfillment, her body demanding, feverishly moving with his as they climbed the spiral of passion together.

She felt suddenly as if she'd been dropped from a great height into a hot, throbbing wave of pleasure that began and never seemed to end. She clung to him, terrified that he might stop, that he might draw back, that he might pull away.

"Shh," he whispered tenderly. "I won't stop. It's all right. It's all right, honey. I love you…so much!"

"I love you, too!" she gasped.

Then he began to shudder, even as she felt herself move from one plane of ecstasy to another, and another, and another, each one deeper and more satisfying than the one before. At one point she thought she might actually die from the force of it. Her eyes closed and she let the waves wash over her in succession, glorying in the unbelievably sweet aftermath.

Above her, Jordan was just reaching his own culmination. He groaned harshly at her ear and shuddered one last time before he collapsed in her arms, dead weight on her damp, shivering body.

"And you were afraid," he chided in a tender whisper, kissing her eyes, her cheeks, her throat.

She laughed. "So that's how it feels," she said drowsily. "And now I'm sleepy."

He laughed with her. "So am I."

"Will you be here when I wake up?" she teased.

He kissed her swollen mouth gently. "For the rest of my life, honey. Until the very end."

Her arms curved around him and she curled into his powerful body, feeling closer to him than she'd ever felt to another human being. It was poignant. She was a whole woman. She was loved.

"Until the very end, my darling," she repeated, her voice trailing away in the silence of the room.

She slept in his arms. It was the best night of her life. But it was only the beginning for both of them.

*   *   *   *   *

Back by Popular Demand!

*Coming in June 2004,
the Mira Books paperback release of*
LAWLESS
by
New York Times *bestselling author*
DIANA PALMER

*With their jointly owned ranch on the verge
of bankruptcy, hard-edged Texas Ranger
Judd Dunn wed Christabel Gaines in name
only, vowing to ignore the sexual tension that
sizzled between them. After all, an innocent
woman like Crissy was off-limits for a man
with Judd's blemished past. Especially a man
who risked his life for a living and had little
regard for matters of the heart.*

*Now, five years later, their futures became
further intertwined when threats of murder
and sabotage turned their lives upside down.
Against all odds, they had to band together
to confront their darkest demons, their new
rivals and their deepest desires....*

*Turn the page for an excerpt from this
riveting tale from a legendary storyteller!*

Chapter One

It was a blistering hot day in south Texas, even for early September. Christabel Gaines was wearing a low-cut white top with faded blue jeans, a book bag slung casually over one shoulder. The top outlined her small, firm breasts and the jeans clung lovingly to every softly rounded line of her young body. The faint breeze caught her long blond hair in her pretty bow-shaped mouth, against her wide forehead and high cheekbones. She moved the strands away, her big, warm brown eyes amused at something one of the students with her was saying about a classmate. It was a long, dull Monday morning.

Debbie, a girl in her computer class, was suddenly staring past Christabel toward the parking lot. She whistled softly. "Well! I know what I want for Christmas," she said in a loud whisper.

Teresa, another classmate, was also staring. "Hubba, hubba," she said with a wicked grin, wiggling her eyebrows. "Anybody know who he is?"

Curious, Christabel turned around to see a tall, darkly handsome man walk gracefully across the lawn toward them. He was wearing a cream-colored Stetson jerked down over his eyes. His neat long-sleeved white cotton shirt was fastened with a turquoise bola tie. His long, powerful legs were encased in gray slacks, his feet in gray hand-tooled boots. On his shirt pocket, a silver star in a circle glittered in the sunlight. Across his lean hips, a brown leather holster and gunbelt were fastened. In the gunbelt was a .45 caliber Ruger Vaquero pistol.

"What have you girls done?" one of the boys asked with mock surprise. "The Texas Rangers are after somebody!"

Christabel didn't say a word. She just stared with the others, but her dark eyes twinkled as she watched him stride toward her with that single-minded determination that made him so good at his job. He was the sexiest, most wonderful man in the world. She owed him everything she had, everything she was. Sometimes she wished with all her heart that she'd been born beautiful, and maybe then he'd notice her the way she wanted him to. She smiled secretly, wondering what the other girls would say if they knew her true relationship with that dynamic Texas Ranger.

Judd Dunn was thirty-four. He'd spent most of his life in law enforcement, and he was good at it. He'd been with the Texas Rangers for five years. He'd been up for promotion to lieutenant, but he'd turned it down because that was more of an administrative job and he liked field work better. He kept that long, lean body fit by working on the ranch, ownership of which he shared with Christabel.

He'd been made responsible for her when she was only sixteen. The D bar G Ranch had been run-down, flat-busted and ready to crash and burn. Judd had pulled it out of the red and made it show a profit. Over the years, he'd put his own money into enlarging the crossbreed beef cattle herd they oversaw. With his canny business sense and Christabel's knowledge of computers, they'd been just beginning to show a small profit. It had allowed Christabel to work on her diploma in computer programming, and Judd even had an occasional spending spree. His last, a year ago, involved that cream-colored Stetson slanted over his dark brow. It did suit him, she had to admit. He looked rakishly handsome. Sadly, there hadn't been any spending sprees this year. There had been a drought and cattle prices had dropped. Times were hard again, just when they'd been looking up.

Any other man would have noticed with amusement the rapt stares of Christabel's two pretty companions. Judd paid them the same attention he'd have given pine straw. He had something on his mind, and nothing would divert him until he'd resolved it.

He walked right up to Christabel, towering over her, to the astonishment of her classmates.

"We've had an offer," he said, taking her by the upper arm as impersonally as he'd have apprehended a felon. "I need to talk to you."

She was escorted forcibly to a secluded spot underneath a big oak tree while her companions watched with wide-eyed curiosity. Later, she knew, she was going to be the focus of some probing questions.

"Not that I'm not glad to see you," she pointed out when he released her, away from prying ears, "but I only have five minutes…!"

"Then don't waste them talking." He cut her off abruptly. His voice was deep, dark velvet, even when he didn't mean it to be. It sent delicious shivers down Christabel's spine.

"Okay," she conceded with a sigh. She held out her hand, palm-up.

He noted the signet ring—his signet ring—that she always wore on her ring finger. Although she'd had it resized, it was still too big for her slender hand, but she insisted on wearing it.

She followed his gaze and flexed her hand. "Nobody knows," she said. "I don't gossip."

"That would be the day," he agreed, and for just an instant, affectionate humor made those deep-set black eyes twinkle.

"So, what's the problem?"

"It's not a problem, exactly," he said, resting his right hand lazily on the butt of the pistol. The Texas Ranger emblem was carved into the maple wood handle. "We've had an offer from a film crew. They've been surveying the land around here with a representative from the state film commission, looking for a likely spot to site a fictitious ranch. They like ours."

"A film crew." She bit her full lower lip. "Judd, I don't like a lot of people around," she began.

"I know that. But we want to buy another purebred herd sire, don't we?" he continued. "And if we get the right kind, he's going to be expensive. They've offered us thirty-five thousand dollars for the use of the ranch for a few weeks' filming. That would put us over the top. We could even enlarge our electric fencing and replace the combine."

She whistled. That amount of money seemed like a fortune. She wondered what it would be like to be rich and have anything she wanted. The ranch that had belonged jointly to his uncle and her father was still a long way from being prosperous.

"Stop daydreaming," he said curtly. "I need an answer. I've got a case waiting."

"It's the homicide, isn't it?" she asked excitedly. "The young woman in Victoria who was found with her throat cut, lying in a ditch with only a blouse on. You've got a lead!"

"I'm not telling you anything."

She moved closer. "Listen, I bought fresh apples this morning. I've got stick cinnamon. Brown sugar." She leaned closer. "Real butter. Pastry flour."

"Stop it," he groaned.

"Can't you just see those apples, bubbling away in that crust, until it gets to be a nice, soft, beautiful, flaky…"

"All right!" he ground out, glancing around quickly to make sure nobody was close enough to hear. "She was the wife of a local rancher," he told her. "Her husband's story checks out and she didn't have an enemy in the world. We think it was random."

"No suspects at all?"

"Not yet. Not much trace evidence, either, except for one hair and a few fibers of highly colored cloth that didn't match the blouse she was wearing," he said. He glared at her. "And that's all you're getting, apple pie or no apple pie!"

"Okay," she said, giving in with good grace. She searched his lean, handsome face. "You want us to let the movie company move in," she added with keen perception.

Nodding, his dark eyes slid over her pretty figure and he got an unexpected and rather shocking ache from looking at her soft curves. He dragged his eyes back up to meet hers. "I'll tell the film company they can come on down, then," he said.

She studied him with admiration. "You do look really sexy, you know," she said. "Tell you what, if you buy me a see-through red nightie with lace, I'll wear it for you," she teased.

He refused to let himself picture her that way. "I told you five years ago, and I'm telling you now," he said firmly, "nothing of that sort is ever going to happen between you and me. In two months you'll be twenty-one. You'll sign a paper, and so will I, and we'll be business partners—nothing more."

She searched his black eyes with the familiar excitement almost choking her. "Tell me you've never wondered what I look like without my clothes," she whispered. "I dare you!"

He gave her a look that would have fried bread. It was a look that was famous in south Texas. He could back down lawbreakers with it. In fact, he'd backed her own father down with it, just before he went for him with both big fists.

But she wasn't intimidated. Not in the least....

Carnival Elation
7-Day Exotic Western Caribbean Itinerary

DAY	PORT	ARRIVE	DEPART
Sun	Galveston		4:00 P.M.
Mon	"Fun Day" at Sea		
Tue	Progreso/Mérida	8:00 A.M.	4:00 P.M.
Wed	Cozumel	9:00 A.M.	5:00 P.M.
Thu	Belize	8:00 A.M.	6:00 P.M.
Fri	"Fun Day" at Sea		
Sat	"Fun Day" at Sea		
Sun	Galveston	8:00 A.M.	

TERMS AND CONDITIONS

PAYMENT SCHEDULE:
50% due upon booking. Full and final payment due by July 26, 2004.
Acceptable forms of payment are Visa, MasterCard, American Express, Discover and checks. The cardholder must be one of the passengers traveling. A fee of $25 will apply for all returned checks. Check payments must be made payable to **Advantage International, LLC** and sent to: **Advantage International, LLC, 195 North Harbor Drive, Suite 4206, Chicago, IL 60601.**

CHANGE/CANCELLATION:
Notice of change/cancellation must be made in writing to Advantage International, LLC.

Change:
Changes in cabin category may be requested and can result in increased rate and penalties. A name change is permitted 60 days or more prior to departure and will incur a penalty of $50 per name change. Deviation from the group schedule and package is a cancellation.

Cancellation:
181 days or more prior to departure	$250 per person
121—180 days or more prior to departure	50% of the package price
120—61 days prior to departure	75% of the package price
60 days or less prior to departure	100% of the package price (nonrefundable)

U.S. and Canadian citizens are required to present a valid passport or the original birth certificate and state issued photo ID (driver's license). All other nationalities must contact the consulate of the various ports that are visited for verification of documentation.

We strongly recommend trip cancellation insurance!
For further details call 1-877-ADV-NTGE or visit www.GetCaughtReadingatSea.com

---

For booking form and complete information
go to www.getcaughtreadingatsea.com
or call 1-877-ADV-NTGE

Complete coupon and booking form and mail both to:
Advantage International, LLC
195 North Harbor Drive, Suite 4206, Chicago, IL 60601

Harlequin Enterprises Ltd. is a paid participant in this promotion.

Visit us at www.eHarlequin.com

GCRSEA2

If you enjoyed what you just read,
then we've got an offer you can't resist!

Take 2 bestselling love stories FREE!

Plus get a FREE surprise gift!

Clip this page and mail it to Silhouette Reader Service

IN U.S.A.
3010 Walden Ave.
P.O. Box 1867
Buffalo, N.Y. 14240-1867

IN CANADA
P.O. Box 609
Fort Erie, Ontario
L2A 5X3

YES! Please send me 2 free Silhouette Romance® novels and my free surprise gift. After receiving them, if I don't wish to receive anymore, I can return the shipping statement marked cancel. If I don't cancel, I will receive 6 brand-new novels every month, before they're available in stores! In the U.S.A., bill me at the bargain price of $21.34 per shipment plus 25¢ shipping and handling per book and applicable sales tax, if any*. In Canada, bill me at the bargain price of $24.68 plus 25¢ shipping and handling per book and applicable taxes**. That's the complete price and a savings of at least 10% off the cover prices—what a great deal! I understand that accepting the 2 free books and gift places me under no obligation ever to buy any books. I can always return a shipment and cancel at any time. Even if I never buy another book from Silhouette, the 2 free books and gift are mine to keep forever.

209 SDN DU9H
309 SDN DU9J

Name	(PLEASE PRINT)	
Address	Apt.#	
City	State/Prov.	Zip/Postal Code

* Terms and prices subject to change without notice. Sales tax applicable in N.Y.
** Canadian residents will be charged applicable provincial taxes and GST.
   All orders subject to approval. Offer limited to one per household and not valid to
   current Silhouette Romance® subscribers.
   ® are registered trademarks of Harlequin Books S.A., used under license.

SROM03   ©1998 Harlequin Enterprises Limited

COMING NEXT MONTH

#1722 THE BLACK KNIGHT'S BRIDE—
Myrna Mackenzie
The Brides of Red Rose
Susanna Wright figured a town without men was just the place
for a love-wary single mom to start over, but then she ended up
on former bad boy Brady Malone's doorstep. Despite the fact
that Brady's defenses rivaled a medieval knight's armor, he
agreed to help the delicate damsel in distress. Now she planned
to help this handsome recluse out of his shell—and into her
arms!

#1723 BECAUSE OF BABY—Donna Clayton
Soulmates
Once upon a time there was a sexy widower whose precious
two-year-old daughter simply wouldn't quiet down. Suddenly
a beautiful woman named Fern appeared, but while she calmed
his cranky child, she sent *his* heart racing! Paul Roland knew it
would take something more magical than a pixie-like nanny to
bring romance into his life. But magic didn't exist…did it?

#1724 THE DADDY'S PROMISE—Shirley Jump
Anita Ricardo wanted a family but Mr. Right was nowhere
to be found—enter the Do-It-Yourself Sperm Bank. But
the pregnant self-starter's happily-ever-after wasn't working
out—her house was falling apart, her money was gone and
Luke Dole was turning up everywhere! She agreed to tutor
the handsome widower's rebellious daughter, but *Luke* was
the one teaching her Chemistry 101….

#1725 MAKE ME A MATCH—Alice Sharpe
When Lora Gifford decided to sidetrack her matchmaking
mother and grandmother by hooking them up with loves of
their own, she never counted on infuriating, heart-stopping,
sexy-as-sin veterinarian Jon Woods sidetracking her from her
mission. Plan B: Use kisses, caresses—*any means possible!*—
to get the stubborn vet to make his temporary stay permanent.